INNOCENCE ENDS

NIKOLAS P. ROBINSON

UNCOMFORTABLY DARK HORROR

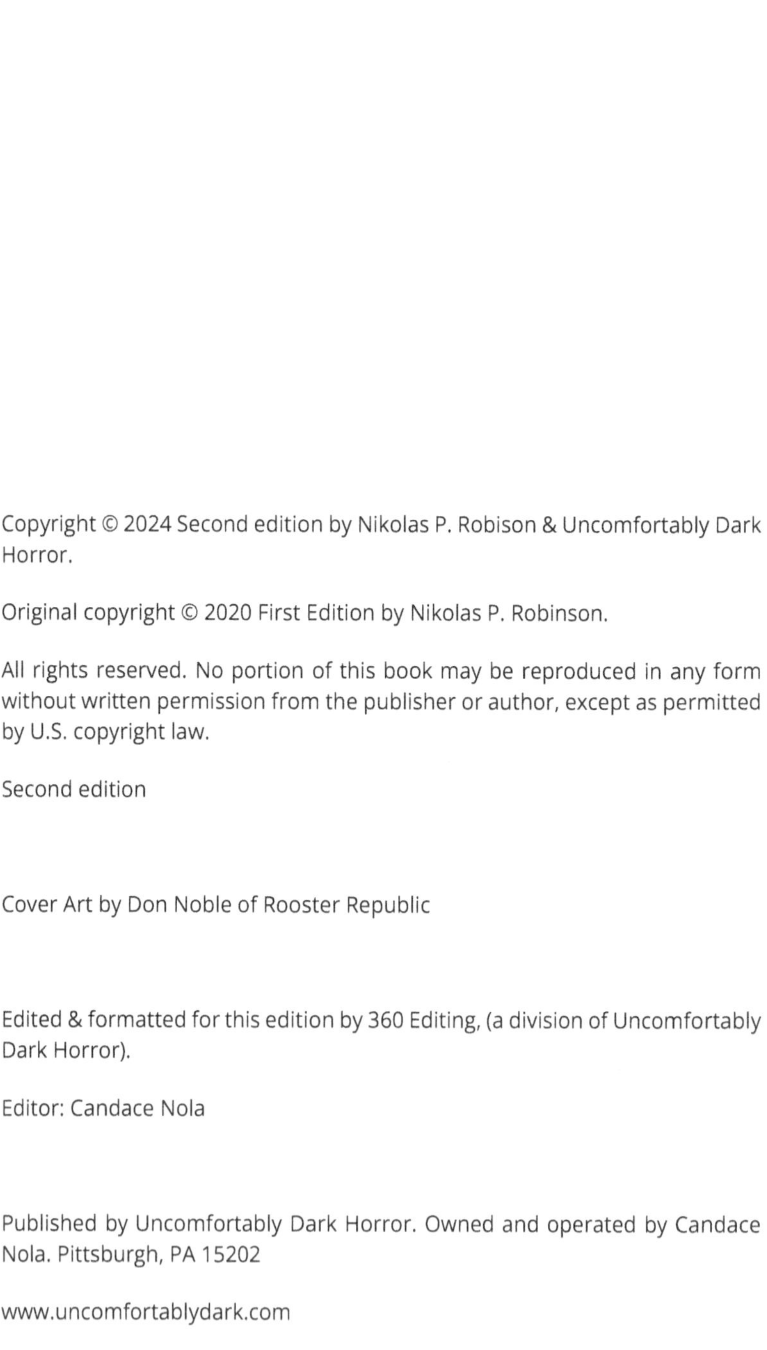

Cover Art by Don Noble of Rooster Republic

Edited & formatted for this edition by 360 Editing, (a division of Uncomfortably Dark Horror).

Editor: Candace Nola

Published by Uncomfortably Dark Horror. Owned and operated by Candace Nola. Pittsburgh, PA 15202

www.uncomfortablydark.com

PRAISE FOR INNOCENCE ENDS

"Nikolas Robinson beckons us to ground zero, where survival is the exception against an infected populace rapidly advancing in number and slaughter. Innocence Ends is a brutal, bloody, and all-too-human view of the last days. This is the way the world ends...not with a bang, but a bludgeon." — Ryan Harding, author of Transcendental Mutilation

"Robinson has grown with each release, proving he's a force to be reckoned with. This polished re-release of INNOCENCE ENDS shows how far he's come, and where he's capable of going. The only thing holding him back is an actual apocalypse!" — Thomas R. Clark, author of Bella's Boys and SummerHome

"Hands down the best zombie story I've EVER had the pleasure of reading! This one would make the

late, great George A. Romero proud!"— Stuart Bray, author of The Blade in the Bath

"Nikolas Robinson is one of indie horror's best-kept secrets." — Lucas Mangum, Splatterpunk Award-nominated author of Barn Door to Hell and Saint Sadist

"Nikolas P. Robinson might possibly be the Neil Gaiman of extreme horror." — Carver Pike, Splatterpunk Award nominated author of The Slaughter Box

"Armed with luminous prose and vivid characterization, Robinson is a powerhouse of a writer. INNOCENCE ENDS is a masterful take on a classic trope. Feast your brains on this one — Brian Bowyer, author of Old Too Soon

CONTENTS

DEDICATION

To Jesse: Thank you for the time you spent listening to my ideas for this story and for reading multiple early edits and providing me with your input and suggestions.

To Jeff: Your initial comments and criticisms of flaws in the writing helped me to polish up something that I feel might be worth sharing with other readers.

To Chandra: Years ago, you encouraged me to write this book after I spent a significant amount of time describing the concepts that led to what I've now completed.

To James: A couple of decades ago, you and I talked about how much we wanted to see the old B-movie trope of vacationers caught in a nightmare brought about by a mad scientist. That conversation from a long time ago planted the seeds for this book.

To Jasmine, Sadie, Vieve, and everyone else who provided me with encouragement and support along the way, your role in this actually being written can't be overstated.

INTRODUCTION

Before you dive into this story, I want to share my thoughts on it, and on why this was such an important project for Uncomfortably Dark. I read this story a while back, maybe shortly after releasing my first novel, and it made me love the zombie trope again.

Before I took a chance on my own writing, I spent almost two decades, if not more, reading and watching every zombie book, movie, and show that I could get my hands on. I have read storylines that included every plot imaginable, including man-made viruses gone wrong, biological warfare, sweeping end of days stories and nuclear wars that brought about mutations, and blood-borne infections that reduced mankind to feral savage creatures.

You name it; I read it, but then I noticed something, a pattern. After the initial factor that creates the undead or zombified being, every story began to feel the same. Same types of characters, same motivations, same situations, same shock-inducing scene, even the same gore. I grew bored and unsatisfied. I had finally reached my breaking point with the concept that I had loved for so long and put the zombie books and movies away.

It made me sad, truly sad, because the zombie storyline had been my thing for so long and I felt like it was coming to an end. I even have a zombie novel of my own, penned across several notebooks that are now gathering dust in a corner. Then I came across INNOCENCE ENDS.

I did not know Nik when I read this one, only had heard of his work within the community and had read a couple of his short stories. I went into this one completely blind. Yes, that is correct. I did not know this was a zombie story. This is the story I might have written, if I had the idea.

It has such an unexpected vibe to it, fresh characters with a nostalgic feel to them. A storyline that unfolds so masterfully, so adeptly that you are in the thick of things without realizing what is happening, but once you are there, it is such non-stop action that it leaves you breathless. This is what a zombie story should be, especially one for modern day.

For those of you that like comparisons, if Stephen King's *'The Body'*, meshed with *'Silent Hill'* and *'Train to Busan'*, you might come close to a little of what this story encapsulates. For those of us that grew up watching the classics like *Night of the Living Dead* and *Dawn of the Dead*, to the more modern *World Word Z, Zombieland*, and *Train to Busan*, and spent hours discussing their survival plan for the zombie apocalypse, this is a must read. For those of us that have always felt exiled to the edges of society and wondered what it would be like to experience such an event, to envision who we would be or wondered if we would survive, this is a must read.

Having gotten to know Nik over the last few years and hearing how the book did not get the chance it should have, having been released in the heart of the Covid lockdown, I wanted to help get it back out there. There are zombie lovers all over the world; whether they see it as a guilty pleasure, a fantasy to escape into and safely reinvent oneself, or a study of the state of the world and all that is wrong with it, I think this story will bring them out of the woodwork, wanting more, falling in love with the trope all over again, like I did.

-Candace Nola, June 2024
Creator of Uncomfortably Dark Horror

1

Chapter One

Tristan Mullins and his best friend, Hewitt Chambers, had been regulars at the Silver Sage Lounge for many years, drinking themselves into a stupor all through their 20s and into their 30s. Countless weekend nights ended with the two of them stumbling down the sidewalks to one or another's home. There they would both pass out while watching late-night horror flicks or playing video games, sleeping frequently until the following afternoon.

Mariah Ehrlich, Hewitt's high school sweetheart, had joined them plenty of times when she wasn't swamped with homework as a college student or drowning in the endless barrage of other people's homework once she'd become a professor herself.

Gale Price used to come around, especially after his parents had passed, until he'd gotten too caught up with his education and his subsequent work with the Centers for Disease Control.

Occasionally Miles Williams and Kateb Abidi would surprise them with a visit, and they would spend a weekend drinking and cavorting, reminiscing about the glory days of childhood.

Abraham Kelly stopped coming around after he'd gotten married and thrown himself into his architectural career.

Growing up together in the same suburb with a pretense of being a city, these seven friends had all gotten drunk many times together. Until now, most of them had not gotten together in this landmark bar at the same time since only a few of them had remained in the area until after they'd turned twenty-one, and there would no longer be a chance of all seven being together again. Tristan's passing guaranteed the whole group could never come together again.

The lighting is subdued, and the music is turned down low in honor of the gathering taking place for one of the bar's long-time patrons.

The six friends sit around the table together, in the same familiar pattern they'd formed at the gravesite, leaving a seat empty for their missing friend, drinking as much as the situation merits, which is quite a bit.

The evening had started somber enough, and quiet. The conversation felt forced and awkward after the funeral, burial, and reception had taken their toll on all of them. The only thing any of them had wanted to do at first was drink and avoid talking about the elephant in the room, what had happened with Tristan. The conversation felt banal and pointless, after all the fake smiles, uncomfortable interactions, pleasantries, and small talk earlier in the day.

An hour later and a few drinks into their night Hewitt decides they've been solemn long enough, "Well, here we all are, for the first time in nearly twenty years, gathered in our hometown, and we're staring at a table and drowning our sorrows. This is definitely not what Tristan would have wanted from us tonight."

"You're right, man," Miles says with a smile. "We got all that sad shit out of the way. It's time to try to be happy."

"Emphasis on try," Mariah says, raising her glass in a mock toast, her red hair continuing to slip from the bun she'd had it tied back in for the funeral.

The conversation gradually develops from that, in fits and starts, hardly flowing or smooth at first, but picking up until, just as gradually, the whole group begins to find comfort in one another again and finally feeling relaxed. Their voices pick up, reminiscing about life years before and catching up on everything since they've all grown up.

They don't forget what brought them all together, but they do begin to focus more on the fact that they are together, setting aside the impetus behind it.

Though they have always tried to remain in touch over the years, this sort of opportunity for catching up isn't something to be neglected or passed up. It's bittersweet to be together the way they are, incomplete, but they all know Tristan wouldn't have wanted them sitting around commiserating and sad. While there had been a deep reservoir of sadness within their friend, it was never something he shared or put on display.

Hewitt had witnessed it in Tristan, on occasion, only because the two of them had spent so much time together and the veneer of joviality and carelessness wasn't perfect, as near as it might have been. It could have had just as much to do with the fact that Tristan and Hewitt had always been the most able to relate to one another, that Hewitt was in tune with things the others might have missed.

Devastated and shattered as he may be, Hewitt was the least surprised when the news of Tristan's suicide reached him.

As much as they might be trying to avoid the elephant in the room, one truth about elephants is that they can only be disregarded for so long. A couple more drinks into their night leads them from the warmth of reminiscence to the depressing topic they know they need to tackle.

"I blame this bullshit, capitalist oligarchy," Gale asserts, pausing to shift his glasses. "If you ask me, it's the world we live in that failed Tristan."

"Whatever you say, Marx," Miles replies with a genuine laugh. "I'm pretty sure you're working for 'The Man' just like I was for a long time there, like a few of us have."

"Gale's right though," Kateb interjects, "this country, maybe even the whole world, doesn't care for individuals who are different or not cut from the standard mold. You know, unless they can be marketed and mass-produced for wide-scale consumption by the masses."

Miles and Kateb glance at each other pointedly, the expression carrying volumes of words left unsaid, leaving Hewitt and Mariah to wonder if this is an argument the two have had in the past.

Miles shifts his gaze from Kateb to Mariah. "What say you, professor? You are, after all, the distinguished representative of the commie elite at our table."

The whole group laughs until they can hardly breathe.

Finally, after catching their breath, the conversation resumes. Mariah never bothering to respond to the dig at her being entrenched in academia.

"I'm totally serious here," Gale continues as if he'd never been interrupted.

"We know you are," Miles replies.

"You always are," Hewitt chimes in with a smirk.

"Stop being assholes for a second and think about it. All of those movies we grew up watching, things like Mad Max, Dawn of the Dead, 28 Weeks Later, and so on, you remember all of that. Those movies showed a world Tristan could have thrived in."

"Those movies, of course, are fiction, Gale," Hewitt says. "Of course, those movies also all show us some awful hellscape of a world too, so I'm not quite sure what your point might be."

"As much as my career depends on that fiction," Mariah responds, "I have to side with Hewitt here. Apocalyptic themes have always been part of our various cultures. They're narratives that have been designed to influence morality, poke and prod at faults in society or the ruling class, or to provide entertainment. Admittedly, the latter seems to be a far more recent thing."

"Red Dawn is more likely, my friend, and I say that as someone who spent years in various war zones," Miles adds. "But that's still pretty far-fetched."

"Miles isn't wrong there," Kateb adds.

"I know how unlikely it is," Gale responds with a self-effacing grin, but his tone implies a seriousness that seems out of place concerning the topic. "I'm just saying that some of us would manage to be better off if the world was more like that fiction we grew up with and loved so much."

Mariah chuckles, "I don't think anyone would be better off in any of those scenarios."

"She is the expert," Kateb adds.

"Hear, hear!" Miles says, and everyone at the table but Gale hits their glasses or bottles against the table in rhythm.

Seeing the downtrodden look on his friend's face, Hewitt interjects, "Hey, let's think this through. Maybe Gale is right," he says. "How many years did we spend fantasizing about various post-apocalyptic scenarios?"

"Thank you, Hewitt," Gale replies, raising his glass with a wink.

"We were children, though," Mariah says.

"Some of us still apparently are," Miles replies without a beat, gesturing to both Hewitt and Gale with his nearly empty beer bottle. "No offense."

"Fuck you too," Hewitt says. "None taken."

"What are your thoughts on the matter, Abraham?" Miles asks. "As the only one of us with a child of their own."

"I think I'd best stay out of this one," Abraham replies. "But, in a pinch, I think I'd probably trust Ben to babysit Hewitt if need be."

Hewitt winces, "Ouch. You hardly have anything to say all night, and this is what happens when you do finally speak up?"

"Better to approach the world with some semblance of child-like wonder and open to possibilities than cynical and jaded," Gale adds with a chuckle. "Also, no offense taken."

"I prefer to think of myself as more jaded than cynical," Mariah replies.

The conversation continues and they spend a while longer reminiscing about their favorite movies and books, moving on to talk about newer material that fits into those same themes. Hewitt and Mariah bring up video games as well, eliciting laughter and mockery from the rest of their friends.

"Hey," Mariah defends herself, "it's research for me. I don't know what his excuse is." She gestures to Hewitt and bats her eyelashes.

"Perpetual adolescence," Hewitt spits out without a pause.

The table erupts in laughter again.

"Besides," Hewitt continues, "I'm pretty sure it wasn't researching when you were sitting around playing Fallout games with Tristan and me. I'm not familiar with any re-search methodology that includes alcohol, sleep-deprivation, and taking over your boyfriend's Xbox for what we'll call an undisclosed amount of time."

"Trade secret, asshole." She playfully slaps Hewitt on the shoulder.

The bartender doesn't rush to usher the group out at closing time, but they finally let the conversation taper off and make their way to the sidewalk outside.

They say their goodbyes and share heartfelt embraces.

Mariah returns to Hewitt's place with him, and Gale follows along. The others make their way to the motel to sleep before they have to begin their drive or catch their flight the next day.

The following morning, the group returns to their real lives, still sad over the loss but refreshed from the time they had together.

They remain in touch, but like before, life gets in the way a lot.

Tentative plans are made to get together like this again, but the logistics aren't in their favor and nothing concrete is established by the time they've all gone their separate ways.

Phone calls and emails are made to suffice in most cases and those who already spent time together continue to do so just like they always had. Hewitt and Mariah do manage to see each other more often, largely because she knows how alone Hewitt is feeling without Tristan there, and Miles and Kateb routinely find themselves in the same places and consider that a happy accident. Gale disappears for long periods, but that's no surprise to any of them. It's the way he's always been.

Just like that, they return to their old routines.

2

Chapter Two

Five Years Later

THE WOODS ARE STILL; dark and silent in that transitional phase before dawn breaks the horizon. Mariah always insisted that she and Hewitt be out in the wild no later than 5 AM when they were hunting.

It was a habit she'd picked up from her father, who had learned it from his father, and she carried it over into her own adult life.

Hewitt never complained about it, not really, though he loved to give her shit about dragging him out of bed so early. There is something tranquil and cathartic about being in the forest, as the natural world was waking with the sun. Regardless of whether they were close to home or vacationing half the country away, these hunting trips with her were things he always looked forward to.

As much as they enjoyed it when other friends could join them, they both preferred the times when it was just the two of them.

Neither of them had even attempted to date anyone else since high school, but years later they still haven't applied any labels to whatever it is they have. Hewitt taunts her, on occasion, by calling himself her boyfriend, but even he doesn't apply the label with any sincerity. Some of their friends found it odd, most notably Abraham, but they had all learned just to accept it as being what it was, whatever that might be.

Mariah looked at the hunting trips as welcome breaks from the softness and surreal life she lived in academia.

She had studied history and sociology in college, loving the study of the world and how people found ways to fit into it, as well as all the ways they failed to do so.

In graduate school, she had focused her studies of history on end times that never managed to come about. She was captivated and engrossed with the sheer number of times the world was meant to end, from the earliest recorded history to modern-day prophecies of cult leaders and less fringe doomsayers. The details always varied, when and why being as myriad as the ways it was supposed to happen.

In the academic world, Mariah found herself a largely untapped niche where apocalyptic eschatology was concerned, and she made herself comfortable there. Her Ph. D. dissertation was on the prevalence of end-times myths in modern culture and media and the symbology thereof.

She, just like her friends, had grown up on a diet of apocalyptic and post-apocalyptic fiction, so it seemed only natural that this was the direction her studies and teaching would have taken her.

Hewitt and Tristan, the two who remained closest to home and the undisputed experts on all things *end of days*, at least within her social circle, served as the sounding board for a great deal of the material she taught or published. Those brainstorming sessions were rewarding experiences for all parties involved, but she was the one who got to reap the accolades.

Hunting trips like this were an escape for Hewitt as well, just not from academia, though he had spent almost as long studying in college as Mariah had, he just hadn't stuck with any single major long enough to graduate until he was finally forced to do so by the university after seven years of just bouncing from one thing to another, whatever appealed to him at the time.

What had started as a scholarship to an in-state school ultimately led to him squandering a significant amount of what he'd inherited from his father's life insurance. His mother had passed in childbirth, so he'd never known her beyond photos and what his father shared with him over the years.

The accident that took his father from him at only twenty-one was the fault of a drunk driver and was the major reason Hewitt never drove drunk or allowed his friends to do so. He drank plenty but was always within walking distance of home.

What Hewitt escaped during these trips with Mariah was a life that seemed to be going nowhere. He was always learning new things and studying anything a random impulse prompted him to study. Still, he consistently felt like he was just spinning his wheels.

He didn't necessarily need to work. All he had to worry about were property taxes and the regular monthly bills; but he bounced from job to job, changing things up when he got bored or felt like he'd gotten everything he could hope to get out of the various positions he held.

Plenty of times, he and Tristan went to the same places to work, neither of them caring to stay in one place for too long. Both of them had been in an ever-evolving and never-ending search for their places in the world.

Hunting with Mariah made Hewitt feel in sync with the world, in tune in a sense he didn't feel anywhere else or at any other time. It wasn't just because he was with her, though that certainly didn't hurt. It was that things were simpler without all the day-to-day trappings of civilization. Maneuvering through society was exhausting sometimes, and he needed these breaks.

Gale hadn't been wrong when he suggested that the way of the world was just as much a cause for Tristan's death as anything else. Hewitt couldn't disagree. He felt the same.

Tristan had always seemed to benefit from these hunting adventures as well, probably for the same reasons Hewitt did.

During the trips they'd taken since the funeral, like this one, Hewitt often wondered whether things would have gone any differently if they'd just done this sort of thing more often. He knew it would have helped him remain more at peace and more grounded and he couldn't help but suspect that it would have done the same for Tristan. He knew that was part of Mariah's reasoning for increasing the number of these trips and he appreciated the effort too much to think of the not-so-subtle manipulation as any sort of violation.

3

Chapter Three

The envelope Hewitt pulls from the manilla envelope in his mailbox is heavy in the way only sturdy, expensive fiber stock can be. There's no return address, but the artistically embellished biohazard symbol on the old-fashioned wax seal gives it all away. He's only just been dropped off by Mariah, as she returns home to check her mail and drop off the hunting gear.

Only Gale, fond as he is of his diseases, would send anything through the postal service with that sort of red flag emblazoned on it. It was no surprise that the smaller envelope had been contained within the larger, yellow one. He debates on waiting for Mariah to get back, but that will be easily half an hour he doesn't want to wait. He weighs the pros and cons and ultimately impatience wins the day.

Attempting to open the missive with as much care as he can manage, Hewitt slowly works a letter opener shaped like a dagger beneath the wax, doing his best not to break the seal so much as separate it from the envelope itself.

On black card stock with metallic red lettering is an invitation to an address in Idaho, a town Hewitt's never heard of, which comes as no real surprise. He's never heard of much regarding Idaho. It takes him a little while, zooming in and out for orientation, before he pinpoints where the destination address is in relation to anything else.

According to Google Maps, as best he can tell, the place is an hour and a half northeast of Spokane, WA. Some nondescript town nestled somewhere in the western reaches of the Rocky Mountains.

Hewitt spends the next half an hour crawling down a rabbit hole, a propensity for which he's never quite able to curb. He spends that time researching the destination online through numerous resources out of an obsessive quirk of his personality. There is nothing in his research, as disappointing as he finds that to be, that would explain why Gale would be there or why he would be inviting anyone else to join him.

The phone call later that evening from Mariah confirms for Hewitt that he wasn't the only one Gale had reached out to. She'd received a similar letter and gotten distracted while attempting to get ready to return to his place. They chat about it for a short while, Hewitt filling her in on what he's managed to learn about the little town. They spend a while attempting to figure out what this little mystery might be before they wind up being forced to call Gale and give up on sorting it out for themselves. He waits for Mariah to get to his house before making the call, wanting to be sure she can hear both sides of the conversation over the speaker.

An email comes in from Kateb, informing Hewitt that both he and Miles had received similar invitations—wherever they are at this time. The email from Kateb isn't forthcoming in offering up any details concerning where in the world those two might be. Hewitt has learned not to be particularly disappointed when that sort of information isn't provided. Usually, it meant that they were in one war zone or another, Miles deep in the shit and Kateb assigned as a civilian monitor of some kind, writing up reports for the Department of Defense and making money on the side as a journalist for whatever news outlet wanted his copy. Down the road, inevitably, his friends would track down a story with Kateb's byline in some publication or another and they'd obtain some insight as to where their friends had been and what they'd been doing.

Now that both Miles and Kateb had gone freelance, the secrecy was worse than it had ever been when the two of them had been enlisted. NDAs were more binding than actual military security clearance, where private contractors were concerned. The legal repercussions for violation were more frightening than they had been while the two had been operating directly for Uncle Sam.

Gale had managed to time things perfectly, or he capitalized on his various contacts established during long years of working for the CDC and WHO in order to guarantee that the deliveries would be made simultaneously. Hewitt takes it upon himself to contact Abraham, who, after sorting through the pile of that morning's mail, confirms that the same invitation had arrived at his home. That covered all of them.

There was no way for Hewitt to know who else might have received one of the invitations, as no one knew what outside relationships Gale had going on or what ancillary contacts he might have through the work he notoriously played close to the chest. All any of them could know for sure was that the core group of friends had all been delivered these same messages on the same day.

Mariah finally shows up and Hewitt dials the number. Gale's phone rings through to voicemail. "Hey, it's Hewitt. We got the invites you sent. Give me a call back when you get the chance."

There isn't anything more for him to say and he always hated leaving messages in the first place. Especially with Gale, leaving messages has always been a 50/50 sort of thing as far as whether he even listens to them. Neither of them expects any sort of immediate response, so they go about the rest of the evening as they would have without the mysterious deliveries.

It is almost a week later when Gale finally returns the call, informing Hewitt that his wasn't the only message left that night. Both Abraham and Mariah had also called to find out what the whole thing was all about. They spend no more than twenty minutes on the phone with one another, neither of them particularly caring for small talk or phone calls. Cliff Notes versions of their lives since the funeral are exchanged, snapshot glimpses into each other's goings-on.

Almost five years of elapsed life condensed into Christmas letter caliber broad strokes by both of them. Gale tells him about the home he's had built in the mountains and, though he's been there for years, he wants everyone to visit and spend a week with him. He assures Hewitt there's plenty of room for them all and that he picked the date to celebrate life during the anniversary of their good friend's death. Gale releases the call after informing Hewitt that he'll be calling everyone else as well.

4

CHAPTER FOUR

MILES COULDN'T WAIT TO get away. He wanted to separate himself from his hometown and his family. He was enlisted with the Army before he'd even graduated, and that following summer he went away for basic training.

He thrived in the military, the routine and discipline being precisely the things he was looking for by signing on in the first place. He'd always been the most physical and athletic of his group of friends, and he quickly displayed promise in this new environment.

From infantry, he moved on to jump school for airborne certification.

Without much family and with a single-minded focus, he dedicated himself to the service, never caring where they sent him or for how long. Miles wasn't one for sightseeing, so the new locations didn't matter much to him except for how those locales would impact combat strategies and logistics.

As more widespread information became available with respect to the autism spectrum, his friends would look back on a life spent close to Miles, and they would sometimes tease him about how he fell somewhere on the spectrum. To his credit, he never got angry about it, and he was self-aware enough to suspect that they might be right.

Once Miles was set on a path, he could continue without distraction as long as it took for him to arrive at its end.

The closest he ever got to being distracted during his deployments were those occasions when Kateb met him in Afghanistan. Kateb's Iranian descent and fluency in multiple Arabic dialects guaranteed he was the best fit for his publisher to send to the Middle East. It helped that he was comfortable in combat scenarios and had gone through four years of military service of his own, albeit with the Navy rather than the Army.

While Kateb had only gone into the service for the promised educational benefits, Miles was there to make a career of it, and he was driven to stand out as the best.

Miles was solidly on track for eleven long years until he was twenty-nine.

It was just five months shy of his 12th anniversary with the Army when an insurgent's round penetrated a weak spot in his body armor and punctured his left lung, only an inch away from his heart. An inch was a world of difference when it came to the difference between life and death, but it may as well have meant death for Miles.

Multiple surgeries and some rehabilitation later, he was honorably discharged for medical reasons. Miles was hurting more from the discharge than from the remaining effects of the bullet and his injury. His planned future was cut short only halfway through the duration he planned to remain in the service. While the recovery was long and painful, but ultimately successful, the thought of returning to the civilian world was more painful by far.

Only two months out of rehabilitation with a clean bill of health, Miles was applying to fill a vacancy with one of the numerous private military contractors that had emerged in post-9/11 America. His background check and security clearances weren't any cause for concern.

Miles hit the ground running, deployments of six months or longer, with no more than a month in between. He would have stayed in the field for longer stretches if the company would have let him. The money was much better than the service had ever been, and the firearms permit he obtained allowed him to purchase items the average citizen never could. As an avid collector, Miles was like a child, provided with a blank check made out to Willy Wonka.

During the infrequent times when he caught up with his friends, they were about evenly split between being impressed and mortified by the arsenal Miles had spent his spare time collecting. Mariah was the one most impressed with it. An avid hunter and a bit of a gun nut herself, she felt more envy than anything else on those rare occasions when she could join Miles at the range. Of course, and he would never admit it to his friends, part of the reason he collected the items he did was just to fuck with them.

5

— ◆ —

CHAPTER FIVE

"OFF THE BEATEN PATH, my ass," Hewitt says as he looks around with his eyes blinking away sleep, taking in the scenery devoid of apparent human presence aside from the road on which they are driving and a faint remnant of airline contrails in the sky just above the horizon. "This place is beyond secluded, isolated doesn't even come close to describing what we're seeing here folks."

"No shit," Kateb agrees. "How did he even find this place? And what the fuck would've possessed him to buy a home here?"

"You don't suppose he became some sort of racist over the years, do you?" Mariah asks, a grin subtly appearing at the corners of her lips as she glances sideways at Kateb.

Hewitt smirks, taking the ball and running with it. "There's always that talk about bigots forming little communities over here in Idaho. I remember hearing about one of those asshole cops who beat that King guy down in L.A. moving up here after the trial."

Kateb begins to laugh. The absurdity of the discussion was altogether too humorous for him to retain a straight face. "No fucking way. Gale is way too caught up in his own shit, that crazy little world of his own to ever subscribe to that sort of thing."

Hewitt continues gazing out the window, blinking sleep from his eyes.

It's a beautiful area, he realizes, now that he's taking in the surroundings.

He would never have expected to see anything this magnificent when thinking about Idaho before today. He can see why Gale would have chosen to live here; he has always been the most appreciative of the natural world and the beauty of the world we live in. Gale was the only one of the friends who never cared for hunting.

Hewitt had always assumed some pretty negative things about Idaho, usually relating to the dirt farming racists he'd joked about, transplants from California where too many minorities had put down roots. Instead, he was taken aback by the mountains and verdant growth of all sorts. It isn't at all what he expected, it's almost magical.

As they weave through mountain valleys, he stares through the passenger side window, the trees so much larger than what he's used to seeing. The mountains themselves make him feel insignificant and small; he loves the sensation.

He can only imagine how lovely it's going to be if the light drizzle turns into a proper thunderstorm, as the weather reports suggest.

The drive takes longer than they thought it would, but none of them seem to mind.

Hewitt isn't alone in feeling a sense of awe at just how magnificent the surroundings are. They're all strangers to the area.

Coming to see Gale is turning out to be an excellent vacation, and it was only just starting. As they round a final bend to bring the town into view, Hewitt smiles.

This is going to be a beautiful week.

The low-hanging clouds obscuring the tops of the mountains all around the tiny valley where the town is nestled add a sense of mystery to the place. It is like something out of a movie, looking at it from above as they descend.

The town is quaint, timeless in a sense, with modernity seemingly melded with a world a hundred years in the past, perhaps more. From the distance, Hewitt could take it all in with one glance and it's fantastic.

They cross a simple wooden bridge over a stream with the pretense of being a creek, and it certainly doesn't seem to qualify as the river it's labeled as being. The road threads its way through a largely untouched span of the forest, blocking the view of the town as they approach. The car feels enclosed by the trees around it, similar to what Hewitt's seen in the New Jersey pine barrens, yet somehow more overwhelming.

They weave their way through the dense forest growth for longer than it seems like it should take before another wooden bridge crosses the same stream; and suddenly they are through as if the forest cleared itself away in response to the shared incredulity of the passengers.

At street level, the town appears to be more like a movie set, the dynamic driving the set builders to design a place that could exist at any point in the past thirty years without giving itself away as being from any particular decade.

6

CHAPTER SIX

As BUILDINGS COME AND go, sliding past his window, Hewitt's attention begins to drift away, returning to a familiar memory that always seems to haunt him around this time of year.

He recalls how six friends once stood in a rough semi-circle, gazing down upon the simple box containing the still form of a seventh member of the gathering, a man they'd once known so well that he was almost family to each of them. The expression on their staring faces a confused mixture of love mingled with sadness as well as pity and regret.

Besides the nearly identical expression shared between their faces, these six individuals appear to have almost nothing in common superficially. They do, however, share approximately the same unspoken thought, each of them wondering if this could have been avoided if only they had kept in better contact during the previous few years. Maybe they could have seen this coming, perhaps registering some warning signs that their intermittent conversations had allowed them to somehow overlook.

As often happens, Hewitt's memory of the afternoon flows into a sort of out-of-body perspective and he sees himself standing there, staring down into the hole in the earth that seems somehow ravenous to him, as if it calls for him, still starving for more.

Miles, a tall black man with a disciplined bearing, stands close to Kateb, a shorter man of Middle Eastern descent. To Kateb's left stands Gale, a pale white man with glasses. Further left, Mariah, with her reddish-blonde hair pinned back in a tight bun, stands hand-in-hand with Hewitt, a taller white man with long hair pulled loosely into a tail at the nape of his neck. To Hewitt's left is Abraham, another white man, shorter, but stocky. Lowered slowly into the ground before them, their friend Tristan is being laid to rest.

The service had been small and tasteful, he remembers. It was an intimate affair devoid of ostentatiousness or pointless ritual, with only close friends and family in attendance. The friends in attendance at the service hardly numbered more than the six watching Tristan being lowered into the ground. Their friend had never been particularly outgoing, and since childhood, he hadn't made any new friends beyond the ones he already had growing up.

Only these six people remained at the gravesite to accompany the workers. The rest of the attendees had already cleared out and were either going their separate ways or returning to the family home where a reception was being held.

Only these six people watched as the gravediggers lowered the casket into the hungry earth and Tristan is settled into his final resting place, swallowed by darkness and soil.

At least he's at peace now.

They all think similar thoughts to that, none of them religious to the point they would suspect their friend purchased a ticket to Hell by taking his own life. He's not suffering anymore, they believe, no matter whether that means he's gone on to a better place or simply that he's gone and with him went his pain.

The six friends broke the semicircle and returned to their vehicles as the first dirt was dropped onto the casket. There was nothing more for them there. The reception awaited, and they all dreaded attending, but knew it would be disrespectful and out of character for them to decline.

The car hits a bump and Hewitt's attention is returned to the present surroundings. Only a few seconds had passed while he was lost in recollections.

7

— · —

CHAPTER SEVEN

THE DIRECTIONS TO THE house aren't difficult to follow. With a population of fewer than thirteen hundred people, there isn't an excess of streets to get lost while navigating. It's certainly bigger and more spread out than Hewitt anticipated when reviewing the map view of the place, but three to four hundred families take up some space in addition to the assortment of businesses, most of which seem to be confined to what looks like a fascinating, historical downtown. Hewitt knows Mariah will want to explore the neighborhood when time allows. The look in her eyes as they pass the worn stone storefronts and brick facades gives it all away.

Exploring the local flavor has to wait, though. The four of them have been cramped in the SUV for a long drive across the better part of the country, and between Miles and Kateb taking turns at the wheel, there have been far too few stops to stretch out and work out the kinks. Comfort was, as far and Mariah and Hewitt could tell, too much of a civilian concern for Miles, and Kateb falls right in line; this wasn't to say that the SUV was uncomfortable at all, but no vehicle is meant to be a long-term residence. Getting out of the car is simply the oasis that Hewitt has found himself clinging to for what seems like hours since the last stop for fuel.

They see the house rising from the forest ahead of them and set apart from the surrounding neighborhood by a spacious lawn and, while none of them had any expectations going into the trip, the house surpasses anything they might have anticipated.

"Our boy is living in style out here in buttfuck nowhere," Miles remarks with a grin but sincere admiration in his tone.

"I was thinking the same thing," Mariah laughs.

The rental car out front, in the larger-than-expected driveway, has to be Abraham's, since he'd told them he would be flying into the Spokane airport with his son, Ben. They'd been beaten here by the family man and Miles was just childish and competitive enough to consider this a challenge he somehow failed. If the rental is Abraham's, that would make the immaculate Lexus NX Gale's, and the vehicle certainly doesn't look out of place in front of the house where it's parked.

They begin unloading the luggage from the back after stretching out the kinks and stiffness hard won by long hours on the road. The door opens and Gale is striding down the steps to the driveway by the time the luggage is all out and sitting on the ground.

"It took you long enough," he says, winking knowingly at Miles. "I was starting to worry you got caught in traffic here in our bustling metropolis."

"Bumper to bumper out there," Kateb shouts from the rear of the SUV without any hint of sarcasm or jest in his voice. "It's real dog-eat-dog out there, but the forbearance of our trusty valet served us well."

Glancing at Miles, who looks ready to drop his luggage for a chance to slap him, Kateb doubles down. "Oh, you must pardon my lack of etiquette. Do you perchance have lodging available for our manservant? He's a savage, but a noble one, and he's grown accustomed to the trifles of our civilized lifestyle."

While everyone laughs hysterically, Miles does indeed drop his bags before lunging at his friend and tackling him in the grass beside the driveway. "I'll show you savage, you smarmy cocksucker."

"Pot and kettle, mother fucker, pot, and kettle," Kateb manages to shout back. Struggling to catch his breath between laughing and the exertion of rolling around on the ground with Miles is more than a little challenging.

Kateb relenting, the two men finally stand up, brushing themselves off and grabbing their bags, stifling laughter with mock composure.

Everyone else, still laughing, follows them into the house, Gale closing the door behind him after glancing around the neighborhood nearby, checking to see if anyone happened to be outside.

They're led to the rooms Gale has taken the liberty of assigning to them and fixing up, Mariah with Hewitt and Miles with Kateb, where they drop off their things without unpacking before receiving a tour of the magnificent house.

They find Abraham and Ben on the cantilevered rear deck, suspended over the lawn by at least seven feet, with no stairs leading down. The French doors leading into the den are wide enough that the whole space seems to be one uninterrupted living space while they are open.

"This place is fantastic," Mariah says and there are nods and sounds of affirmation all around.

"It should be," Abraham says, wrapping her up in his huge arms. "I designed this magnificent bastard of a home for our magnificent bastard of a friend. I knew it would be interesting, based on Gale's specifications, but I never really imagined how beautiful it would be with the surroundings, though."

"I did nothing more than describe what I was looking for and provided some details that were important to me, plus I gave him an overview of the landscaping I had in mind," Gale replies. "This genius delivered something awe-inspiring, and he deserves all the credit."

"I thought you'd never been here before?" Hewitt asks.

"I hadn't," Abraham explains. "I designed it and sent the blueprints to the contractor Gale was using locally. I wish I'd built this one myself. Too much on my plate, though."

"Great job, my man," Miles says, whistling with appreciation. "Remind me to keep you in mind when I want a palace of my own."

The group remains outside for a while, enjoying the brisk but nowhere near cold afternoon, playing catch up with one another and filling in the gaps of the previous five years where they haven't had time or availability before. More than an hour passes like this before Gale suggests they head downtown for an early dinner at an establishment there.

"Deal," Miles says, hungrier than he thought he was until the topic of food was brought up. "But I warn you, if any of these people call me 'nigger,' all bets are off."

Hewitt laughs and replies, "I'll take odds that Kateb gets called towel head first."

Kateb raises his hand, "I've got $50 on 'terrorist.'"

Gale interrupts, "Odds are likely that sexual preference will be a bigger hangup than skin tone for both of you." He leaves the silence hanging after his statement, his friends staring at him with varying degrees of discomfort, until he cracks a grin. "Everything's fine and the people here have been great. Let's get going."

"You're driving, Gale," Miles says. "Been on the road for too long."

Gale ushers Miles and Kateb to his Lexus while Hewitt and Mariah climb in with Abraham and his son. The vacation is just beginning, and they already feel the warmth in one another's company that they haven't felt in a long while. So focused on each other, no one notices the looks from some of the people they pass along the way.

8

CHAPTER EIGHT

The diner Gale leads them to is a nice place.

It's nice in the way anything belonging to the previous generation seems nice. The style and theme of the place make it feel like they stepped into a time warp on the way through the door. It was like something from Happy Days or Archie.

Anachronistic is the word that comes to Hewitt's mind as he takes in the surroundings. The interior of the restaurant could have fit in equally well, at any point between the 1950s and the 1980s, more so than the town itself had when he got his first impression. In here, there weren't newer model vehicles to spoil the illusion. Were it not for the fact that the business had existed there the whole time, Hewitt would have considered it to be the most authentic retro establishment he'd seen.

"This place is terrific," he remarks.

Gale nods and smiles. "Wait until you try the food."

The group, led by Gale, makes their way across the tile floor to a couple of tables near the far edge of the dining space. A waitress is already there, joining the two tables together and rearranging the chairs to suit the seven people in the party.

They peruse the menus in silence, content just to be together again under better circumstances than the last time they'd congregated. The only sign of boredom comes from Abraham's son, as he kicks the legs of the chair beneath him while waiting for everyone else to make up their minds.

Orders are gradually placed, and drinks are set in front of them

The catching up continues where it left off before.

Hewitt and Mariah share details of their regular hunting trips over the intervening years, including the mishaps and blunders that provide everyone with a great deal of entertainment. Miles is more forthcoming than he's ever been concerning the places he'd been deployed as a contractor than he ever was during his career with the military. He displays a refreshing sense of openness now that he doesn't have to worry about the phone or email correspondences being monitored.

Kateb similarly displays openness that is refreshing, in some cases supplementing Mile's own stories where they dovetailed in the past. Abraham shares stories of his family and some of the more bizarre aspects of his building contracts. Gale talks about his work with the CDC and WHO, which includes some truly terrifying accidents in lab environments that are humorous only because worst-case scenarios hadn't played out.

As well as they kept in touch under normal conditions, it is still so vastly different to be face-to-face, with no tragedy looming darkly over the gathering. It had been so long since they had all come together before the funeral and during the five years since then. The atmosphere is celebratory, like a holiday known only to them and observed in exclusivity.

The food is the sort of greasy spoon diner fare one can find anywhere in the country, but it is just as delicious as Gale suggested it would be. The years since youth wash away with a tide of happiness and sentimentality.

It's a couple of hours later before they decide, as a group, to retire to Gale's house for the night and further relaxation.

Abraham ushers Ben off to sleep with minimal disagreement from the exhausted boy and returns to the den where the friends are all relaxing with drinks.

———

THAT NIGHT, FILLED WITH good food and warm feelings, the conversation is less animated than while they were at the diner but no less pleasant and engrossing. Back in the comfort of Gale's home, they are lulled into simply feeling relaxed and refreshed, anticipating the rest of their stay being the getaway none of them consciously knew they needed until they'd arrived.

The overlapping conversations last well into the late-night hours; unfettered as they are, without any strained joviality or uncomfortable silences like they would be with any other company.

"We'll be getting up and about for an early start tomorrow morning," Gale finally announces as the clock indicates the approach of midnight. "There's a little spot I have in mind for some fishing, but it's a bit of a hike from here."

"I think I speak for everyone present when I say we're up for it," Mariah confirms.

All around the room, there are nods, assorted grunts, and gestures of affirmation. The day Gale has planned for them, though they don't know the details, sounds like precisely the sort of thing they had been expecting after seeing the gorgeous location Gale had invited them to.

Outside, a light rain begins, the cool air of the night bringing out the moisture taken in by the clouds from the warmth of the day. With the doors to the patio still open, a cool breeze carries with it the smell of rain and pine into the room.

"I can certainly understand why you invited us here," Hewitt says, breathing deep the fresh air and savoring the scent of the place.

"It is my own little bit of paradise," Gale replies wistfully. "What better place to get back to our own better natures than somewhere so thoroughly embedded in nature itself?"

"No argument from me," Mariah chimes in.

Kateb speaks up from where he's slouched in his seat, putting words to something they've all found themselves thinking of at various points throughout the day since they'd arrived. "The place appears to be doing wonders for you, my friend. I don't know that I've ever seen you looking so happy or healthy."

Gale reflects on his friend's comment for a moment, smiling at the compliment. "It's amazing how life-changing it can be when you find your purpose in life and know you're where you belong, doing what you should be doing."

He pauses for a bit, chewing on his words to test the flavor before sharing them. "I'm hoping this week can do the same for all of you as well. Some of you," He nods to Mariah and Abraham pointedly, "Some of you have, without question, found your calling in this world and you've carved out your place in it."

"Some of us, you say?" Miles asks with feigned offense.

"Well," Gale begins, chuckling softly, "I don't imagine being a mercenary was exactly your first choice."

"Contractor," Miles corrects, middle finger punctuation the statement with a grin on his face that displays his amusement. Miles can't begin to tabulate the number of times that same conflation of terms has been applied to him over the years. Kateb makes a habit of doing so just to get under his skin at times, but Miles had never been particularly thin-skinned.

There are chuckles through the room before Gale can continue. The whole group has started laughing and soon sleep-deprivation and road-weary exhaustion have kicked in and they are doing little more than laughing at each other's laughter. It takes a couple of minutes before composure's been regained and by then, the conversation, or at least where it was going, has been lost.

The light-hearted conversation continues for another quarter of an hour until they, as a group, decide it's time for bed.

They expect a long day ahead of them and sleep is already on everyone's minds after the travel and the time they've spent catching up.

Abraham unrolls a sleeping bag for himself, letting Ben have the bed in the room they're sharing.

Kateb closes the door behind them as he and Miles make their way to the bed, undressing one another as they cross the room and only breaking contact between their lips when they can't get their shirts off otherwise. They have both always enjoyed making a mess of new rooms when they stay in them, and the bed Gale's furnished their bedroom with looks to be more comfortable than anything they've experienced outside of high-end hotel suites.

Hewitt and Mariah stifle their amusement, though bare-ly, as they hear the door close to Miles and Kateb's room, grateful that they are a couple of rooms down the hall from those two. As they undress and climb into their bed for the night, there's a mutual, unspoken understanding that they're both too exhausted for the sort of activity currently being enjoyed by their friends. Mariah nuzzles up to Hewitt, her head resting against his chest and his left arm posi-tioned to allow his hand to caress her shoulder lightly with his fingertips. In only a few minutes, she is breathing deeply and snoring just slightly.

Hewitt lies awake, in the almost absolute darkness of the room, enjoying the simple pleasure of feeling her there and hearing the tiny noises she makes in her slumber. This is a routine for them, and a familiar one, since Hewitt's always been plagued with insomnia.

Finally, though, in the early hours of the morning, he does drift away, comforted by the knowledge that he has a lovely week to look forward to and feeling optimistic about how refreshed and revitalized he'll be feeling by the time it's over.

Gale sits awake in his room for a while, consumed by thoughts of work, running through plans in his mind and trying to account for potential shifts in variables he can't control. For him, this isn't so much a sign of stress as his version of counting sheep.

9

Chapter Nine

A scream breaks the silence of the otherwise peaceful ni ght.The desperate, shrill voice echoes off of the walls of nearby homes before dissipating and being lost to the darkness.A door slams savagely, the force of the closure shaking the windows of the house in their frames.This sound doesn't carry quite as far through the neighbor- hood, though it could be heard a couple of houses away if anyone were listening.

A violent banging begins. The repeated detonations of fists against wood and plaster are only barely audible beyond the walls of the house itself. If some curious neighbor were to walk by, meandering down the side- walk in the middle of the night, perhaps they might hear something and wonder what's going on.

No one walks by. No one nearby is curious.

As the crackle and clatter of wood splintering begin to accompany the booming of the blows, a new scream erupts from within the house. Neighbors are listening as the shriek becomes a gurgle, gradually fading to silence, but none of them care. The violence in their midst is drowned out by a different, yet similar sort of violence in their own hearts and minds.

Something darker than the Rocky Mountain night outside has been taking hold of these people. The abrupt escalation within one home is little more than the herald of worse to come.

10

CHAPTER TEN

HEWITT IS THE FIRST to wake in the morning; before any alarms have gone off, he is standing on the rear deck as the sky begins to glow to the East.

Soon, the sky is aflame, though the sun hasn't breached the horizon, the bar set so high by the mountains in all directions. As the others begin moving and preparing for the day ahead, the sunrise plays off of the storm clouds, rolling off to the East and over the mountain peaks, producing the most brilliant display of oranges and reds, hints of pink here and there. In Hewitt's mind, there are beginning to be some astoundingly positive marks in the plus column as far as this secluded community is concerned.

GALE HADN'T BEEN KIDDING when he recommended that everyone needed to pack for the vacation with an understanding that there would be some strenuous hiking involved. Looking around as they'd first approached the destination, they had all started to grasp just what their friend had in mind.

Cutting their way through the dense pine forest on what could only be laughably referred to as a trail, it isn't just Hewitt who worries he had vastly underestimated what Gale meant when he said it would get strenuous.

Miles and Kateb make it look easy enough, but the thin air and high elevation take a toll on even the fittest of the group.

Surprisingly, to all of them, Gale leads the way with seemingly boundless energy and easy enthusiasm. He'd never been the most active or physically capable member of their group, but it was clear, even before the day's adventure, that a lot had changed with their friend. It wasn't until they were out in the woods that the extent of those transformations had become apparent.

The trail they follow is, at best, something worn into the vegetation by wildlife rather than human traffic and Gale is surefooted and quick in his negotiation of the terrain. He'd taken up exercise, and he carries himself with more confidence than any of his friends are accustomed to seeing.

Mariah is happy to see it, though. More than the rest, the years had been good to Gale, and he certainly seems happier and more at peace in her eyes than he had when they'd last gotten together.

Sounding barely winded by the exertions, Gale shouts back over his shoulder, "Not much further to go!"

They have been on the trail for more than an hour, drinking plenty of water and eating snacks while on the go, and they are all looking forward to reaching the secret and mysterious destination Gale has in mind.

The smell of the place is magnificent, Hewitt thinks, the air so clean and the pine strong but not overpowering. The evening rain from the day before has still left the ground sodden in places and the scent of wet earth only adds to the beauty of it.

Gale had started the morning by reiterating to them that this trip was going to be about taking them to simpler times and a world that made more sense. Being out here in the woods with him, not a single argument could be made against the value of that plan.

The sun has only barely started to peek its way over the mountainous horizon as they reach their destination, devouring some of the shadows and enhancing others in the process.

Ahead is a clearing with spring flowers in yellows, purples, and reds dotting the greenery and a pool of the cleanest water Hewitt has ever seen outside of professional nature photos. Stream fed, he sees the downstream waters disappearing into a dense copse of trees.

"This is one of the literally dozens of streams that feed into the river you crossed a couple of times on your way into town," Gale explains, catching where Hewitt's attention is fixed.

"I don't know that I'd call it a river," he replies, smiling.

"Give it time," Gale says. "There's still plenty of snow to melt at the higher elevations as it gets warmer, and early summer can bring a lot of rain to the region."

Hewitt nods, only halfway paying attention to what Gale's saying, silently taking in the beauty of the glade. Mariah approaches Hewitt from behind, hooking her left arm around him and leaning her head against his upper arm. "It's beautiful, Gale," she says.

"Yes, it is," he replies without hesitation. "And the best part is that it is hardly touched by people. I found this little glade a couple of years back and I've never seen a sign that anyone else has ever disturbed this place since then.

Naturally, it helps that the trail begins at the edge of my property."

His words lead to the rest of them taking in the surroundings with a little more eye for detail and even Mariah, the most avid hunter of the group, can't find any obvious indication that anyone else had ever been there before this very moment.

Knowing that Gale has made this trek, and probably many others, over the years he's lived there certainly helps them to understand why he looks so much healthier. Nature and the outdoors had done him a great deal of good, especially combined with the room in his house dedicated to well-used exercise equipment.

"Well, let's unpack and catch some fish," Gale says, smiling like a little boy.

They unpack the gear Gale had prepared for the adventure and the day of fun and relaxation gets started.

The fish aren't all too interested in biting, though they can be seen flitting about beneath the surface of the pool. The friends aren't all too interested in actually catching the fish either. The purpose of the fishing trip isn't to catch anything so much as to enjoy the beautiful day, to take in the peace of the location, and to share each other's company.

Lunch was prepared in advance and hauled out with them, and they eat their meal sitting on exposed stones at the pond's edge with their feet dangling above the water, Mariah going one step further and trailing her bare toes throughout the cold mountain water.

As much as none of them want to leave, in late afternoon they make the return hike back down to Gale's house with less urgency than their trip up the mountain had involved.

Across the board, everyone is not only content but invigorated by the first day of their shared vacation.

Gale is satisfied with himself and the twinkling in his eyes accompanies the youthful smile on his face. The success he perceives the day as having been, he considers silently, is only the beginning. It's only going to get better from here. The journey of bonding and self-discovery has only just started. His friends, blissful and happy, have no idea what remains ahead of them.

11

— · —

CHAPTER ELEVEN

DEPUTY ALBERT WEBER GLANCES up from the crossword he's filling out as he hears the crash of thunder resonating all through the valley, and the ground shakes just enough for him to feel it. This, he can tell, is going to be a real storm, unlike the short-lived rain the night before. He'd suspected as much as he watched the angry clouds roll in over the town while he had driven a final patrol through the streets near dusk.

He's only two days from the end of his week-long stint staying at the Emergency Services Building in town, and he almost dreads heading back down in elevation and returning to work again. The rotating shifts spent here have always felt like a mini-vacation of sorts, time for relaxing and woolgathering, maybe catching up on reading in the process. Mostly he's been reading.

Nothing eventful ever happened in this town. It was a sweet deal, being paid his normal salary to do little more than chat with the locals he's gotten to know over the years and enjoying the fresh mountain air. The people who traditionally kept him company during these shifts haven't been so personable during this interval, but he figures it's some late-season cold or flu keeping them at home. People are never the most sociable when they're under the weather.

He knows he certainly isn't. Besides, the storm probably spells the end to any real chance of socializing during the remainder of his time on shift.

The weather radar he pulls up shows a large mass of clouds clustering just up north in Canada and slowly encroaching on the Rockies. He's used to the weather this time of year and he figures they're in for a couple of days of everything being wet. At least it doesn't look like snow in the forecast, he thinks, though he's sure there's probably going to be a fresh white coat on the peaks in view if he takes a look in the morning. It could stay raining at the higher elevations, but he doubts it at this time of year.

Loud as it is, the thunder never manages to fully awaken Hewitt where he lies on his side, his right arm loosely draped over Mariah's hip. The day had taken such a sufficient toll on him that he fell asleep without any trouble. A dreamless night provides him with much-needed rest.

They're all too tired to do more than approach the tenuous edges of wakefulness in response to the crashes and rumblings outside. No one tucked comfortably in bed at Gale's house even registers that a storm has come.

As dawn makes its feeble attempt to lighten the sky, the rain continues unabated; the clouds seeming content to remain where they were.

12

— · —

CHAPTER TWELVE

SARAH'S BARE FEET SLAP painfully against the wet asphalt as she runs without any destination in mind. If she had her wits about her, she might attempt to make her way across town to the Emergency Services Building, where there's sure to be a Sheriff's Deputy present. In school, she'd had a tour of the building last year and she knew someone from the Sheriff's Department is always there. For the moment, she's just trying to stay ahead of her step-father and step-brother.

If she'd taken her melatonin before bed, she might not have woken up to the meaty thud of the tire iron against her older sister's head. The unfamiliar noise pulled her from the edge of sleep, and she sat up in bed, staring through the dim light intruding from the doorway, trying to make sense of what she was seeing.

She opened her eyes to a silhouette looming over the bed across the room. Uncertain what the noise might have been, she begins to speak just as the silhouette raised its arm; the shape extending beyond what should be the normal length, brushing almost against the ceiling.

"Daddy, is that you?"

The limb descended rapidly, no indication that her step-father might have heard her question.

The wet, splintering pop of the second blow startled Sarah enough that she frantically tucked herself up against her headboard, pulling her nightgown down to cover her bare legs.

Her step-father turned towards her then and in the faint light, she could make out a strange smile on his face as he tucked his right arm behind his back. She recognized him, but she didn't at the same time. Whoever this was, she knew it wasn't really her step-father.

His voice sounded like it always did when he was trying to make believe that he wasn't angry about something. "Hey, sweetheart. What are you doing awake? You were supposed to be asleep like your sister."

"The noise woke me up," she said.

He approached her bed slowly.

A sudden clattering cacophony arose from downstairs, and her mother screamed. "Angela, Sarah, get out of the ho-!"

The final word was cut off by a new burst of noise from what might have been the kitchen.

Sarah didn't wait. She was up and out of her bed before her step-father could bring the tire iron out from behind his back.

She was through the door and down the stairs in only a couple of seconds. She didn't take the time to look through the archway into the kitchen, where her mother lay bleeding on the floor, her body convulsing as her step-brother forcefully dragged the blade of a kitchen knife along the now exposed spine near the base of her skull.

She might have stopped if she'd taken even a moment to glance in there.

She fumbled with the lock for just a moment before opening the front door and bursting into the rainy night outside.

The older boy's scream echoing after her, "Get back here, you little bitch!"

She hasn't stopped running since then, her feet in agony and her lungs burning after only a couple of blocks. Over the sound of the rain and the intermittent thunder, she can hear her step-brother catching up to her. To her left, a woman watches through her window, making momentary eye contact with Sarah just as her pursuer catches her.

He barrels into her from behind, knocking her against the pavement, shattering two of her teeth and crumpling up her nose. The breath left in her lungs explodes out and as she tries to breathe in, she swallows a mouthful of rain and blood, gagging and choking on a piece of tooth that catches on her tonsils.

By the time her step-brother gets off of her, his father has caught up with them and they begin dragging her back toward the house, each taking her by a leg.

She stares hopelessly up at the house along the street where she'd fallen, but the woman standing at the window pulls the curtain closed, leaving Sarah with no one to save her.

13

***

CHAPTER THIRTEEN

"IT ALWAYS RAINS PRETTY steadily this time of year," Gale says, gazing out the window. "It could be on-and-off or it could rain straight through for the next week or two."

Hewitt turns to look at him. "You could have timed this a bit better. Outdoor activities are clearly off the table under these conditions."

"The timing is what it is. The weather wasn't my primary concern. It was the anniversary that mattered."

Hewitt winces slightly—and he hopes, imperceptibly—as he thinks back on the last time they'd all been together.

"You're right," Hewitt says. "Gloomy does seem fitting in its own way."

The two of them continue watching the storm building up outside in silence. Floor to ceiling windows presents them both with a spectacular view even with the rain and low-hanging clouds obscuring the mountains to the East.

Mariah is the only other one already awake, and she beat Hewitt to the guest shower.

"It's beautiful out there," she announces as she enters the den, drying her hair with a towel.

Gale nods in response without saying a word.

Mariah shoves Hewitt's knee from where it had been resting on the loveseat cushion next to where he's sitting and lowers herself down. He absently puts his arm around her and pulls her slightly closer.

"We'll need all of this rain, all of it we can get," Gale says after a long interval of silence. "It gets damn dry around here as summer stretches on. Fire is always a serious possibility and a huge threat."

Hewitt smiles. "Let it rain then."

The sound of droplets hitting the glass and ceiling becomes almost hypnotic for the three of them as time passes by, barely noticed.

Gradually Ben, then Abraham, followed by Kateb and Miles, made their way from where they were sleeping to the den as well. The rain appears to have a similar soothing effect on all of them, as no one appears interested in prolonged conversation or breaking the silence beyond small niceties.

Indifferent to the witnesses inside, the rain falls harder as the day passes.

Clouds build up and prepare to unleash their burden throughout the day.

Gale and Abraham go overboard with the late breakfast, preparing more food than the seven of them can finish, though they do get closer to accomplishing that goal than any of them would have expected.

Friendship and familiarity increase the appetite as much as the recent travel consisting of long days and nights followed by the late-night spent catching up.

With the rain likely to continue, plans to hike the neighboring mountain forests are shelved and a game of Cards Against Humanity is tossed into the mix.

Knowing his friends as he does, Abraham is initially resistant to playing that particular game with his son present.

Ben insists that he's seen worse and heard much worse, including other people playing the same game or others like it while he watched videos on YouTube.

With exaggerated resignation, Abraham finally shrugs and concedes Ben's victory.

Soon enough there are tears of laughter in his eyes and his cheeks feel cramped from the strain the smile is putting on the muscles of his face.

HEAVY RAINS LEAD TO hope for the farmers at lower elevations, hope that the drought of the previous three years might be over as the Farmer's Almanac seemed to claim it would be.

At higher elevations, areas like the valley where the town nestles itself between rising peaks, the rainfall combines with early snowmelt to feed into the numerous streams and rivers.

Every few years, it seems to happen like this. The river strains to overflow its banks, threatening to cover the single road out of town, the sole means of reaching the rest of civilization. Less frequently, any local could verify, the flooding gets so severe that it overflows the road entirely.

Unfortunately for the group of friends gathered together, most of whom have responsibilities out there in the wider world, this storm is contributing to one of those rarer occasions. If the road goes out, it's likely the phone lines will be taken down as well, running, as they do, alongside that path.

The power lines are less susceptible, following their path into town, a cleared path through the otherwise dense trees from the nearest substation.

14

—·—

CHAPTER FOURTEEN

LIGHTS FLICKER INTERMITTENTLY THROUGHOUT the town as the storm grows stronger and the lightning more frequent.

The lawns become saturated and the roads act as aqueducts, carrying water away from the surface and toward drains that empty into the river. Only during times like this does the river manage to live up to its name rather than being the creek the visitors had crossed over twice on their way into town a couple of days before.

Already swollen with the late spring snowmelt, the river expands beyond its banks and churns away at soil along the way, loosening rocks and roots from where they were embedded.

It isn't long before the road is beneath the water at both of the points where it crosses over the normally peaceful stream. Debris collides upstream of the two bridges, gradually accumulating into a dam of sorts, forcing the water to lash at the bridge in ways it wasn't designed to withstand.

Still, it holds up against the abuse.

Both bridges are underwater within the first twenty-four hours of the torrential rain reaching its high point. Within forty-eight hours, the road itself, where there is any sort of trough in place, is similarly submerged. The space between bridges is soon mostly underwater.

The asphalt itself, as well as the bridges, remains mostly structurally sound, but any attempt to traverse that single route from the mountain valley to the outside world would be unsafe, if not outright impossible.

It's Steve Duncan, one of the residents of the town, who discovers the condition of the road as he is heading south to Coeur D'Alene to meet his ex-wife and to pick up his daughter for the summer.

Intent as he is to get through the waters, Steve almost gets swept off the side of the road from the current and as he attempts to safely back away to higher ground, his truck only narrowly avoids being sideswiped by a sizable tree that had either been uprooted or picked up from where it had previously fallen.

If he hadn't started reversing when he did, there would have been an impact.

His heart is racing from the experience, but what he feels is anger rather than fear.

Anger that he hadn't gotten out of town sooner.

Anger that he isn't going to meet his bitch of an ex-wife and will likely never hear the end of how he disappointed their daughter—again. This would be just another thing for her to hold over his head.

Mostly he is angry that he will be stuck in town, separated from his daughter, the only family he cares to see.

He is still stewing in his feelings when he stops at the gas station to warn the idiot behind the counter that the road is out.

His emotional state hasn't improved when he stops in at the Emergency Services building that doubles as a volunteer fire station and County Sheriff's outpost.

Deputy Albert Weber sits behind the front desk, watching as the drenched man slams open the door with apparent irritation. Even before he finished pulling the hood away, the truck gave away the visitor's identity as soon as it pulled up.

"Can I help you, Mr. Duncan?" he asks, his tone of voice not masking the annoyance he feels.

"Fucking road's flooded out before the bridge!" the man responds. The man's glare and attitude are pushing all the wrong buttons for the deputy, who is just now finding out that he won't be looking forward to being relieved in about forty-eight hours as he'd been expecting.

"And you expect me to do what, exactly?"

The man pauses for a moment, exhaling with a derisive huff. "I don't fucking know! Call someone! Get help out here and get up off your ass!"

"Buddy, if the road's out, there's no help getting through," Albert replies, doing his best to remain calm and measured. "Best I can do is spread the word around town and pass the info along to the main office."

Enraged, Steve lunges toward the desk, almost succeeding in making it over the counter between them, but Deputy Weber sees the attack coming and slides his chair to the side on its stiff rollers. He's out of his chair fast enough to tap the irrational lunatic at the base of his skull with his fist as the man slides onto the desktop, trying to stop his forward momentum, dragging numerous items to the floor with him as he falls.

Steve hits the ground hard, and the deputy has the man's arms pinioned behind his back before he's even fully settled into his prone position.

He leverages the stunned local up to his feet and shoves him into one of the two cells available for the Sheriff's office, remnants left behind from when the town was still a successful mining community.

The man begins furiously beating at the bars, opening gashes in his knuckles.

The deputy watches the man curiously for a bit before sneering and returning to his desk. He spends the next few minutes picking everything up, straightening it out, and putting it back in place before grabbing the radio to call in both the road conditions and the subsequent altercation with the man finally calming down in the cell.

He tries to get through multiple times before resigning himself to suspecting that the signal repeaters must have gotten knocked out by the storm. There is no return to his call, only static.

He picks up the phone and dials the county office. As he is relaying the details of the attack from the prisoner, after he'd already advised them of the road closure, the line goes dead.

He tries to get a new tone, checking the hard line's connections before accepting what he knows has happened.

If the road was as badly flooded as the maniac in the cell claimed it to be, it was only going to be a matter of time before the phone line got knocked out as well.

Clearly, this was not going to be his day.

With a glance at his prison, Deputy Weber collects the keys to his cruiser, puts on his coat and leaves the building, locking up behind himself and almost immediately regretting the fact that he's gone out into the rain.

No phones mean that he needs to actively drive from business to business, letting them know the situation concerning both the road out of town and the phone lines. They will spread the word effectively to the rest of the folks so that he doesn't have to go door-to-door.

The last thing he wants is a bunch of accidents or injuries on his watch thanks to residents trying to leave in these conditions.

First things first, though, he needs to put cones out to block the road, far enough back that they won't get swept away by rising floodwaters. One of his counterparts is probably en route to do the same thing at the other end of the affected area.

This sort of thing had happened before, maybe seven years earlier, if he recalls correctly.

Thankfully, he hadn't been on duty back then, but it had taken more than a week before anyone could get through, in part because one of the bridges had been entirely knocked out at that time.

As he stands there in the rain, placing sandbags and orange cones across the road, he wishes to himself that he could just go back home. The thought of staying here in town for another week or even longer is not something he's pleased to imagine.

Maybe, he thinks, *it won't be as bad this time.*

15

Chapter Fifteen

The interior of the bar is dim and country music plays at a subdued volume. This is a blessing for all of them but Abraham, the only one who openly enjoys that style; though Kateb secretly considers it a guilty pleasure of sorts and finds himself tapping his feet unconsciously to the rhythm. The bar is imbued with the sort of rustic ambiance that seems entirely fitting there in the Western foothills of the Rocky Mountains. The country music seems as natural as the unpolished woodgrain of the tabletop around which they sit.

While they do get loud on occasion, eliciting sideways glances and intermittent glares from the other patrons, everyone else in the bar keeps to themselves, including the waitress carrying their drinks from the bar.

Gale and Abraham stick to soda, for the most part, being nominated as designated drivers. Abraham opted for a single beer upon first arriving, knowing that it will be out of his system by the time they get around to leaving.

Ben sits back and enjoys being treated like one of the adults, interjecting his thoughts in the conversations as he gradually becomes more comfortable with his new status among his father's friends, no longer thinking of them as strangers. Aside from a bitter sip from his father's beer, which led to his face contorting in ways the rest of the group found hilarious, Ben also spends the evening drinking soda.

Hours pass as they enjoy the drinks and the company; Hewitt most of all, feeling for the first time in a while as if he is with family. For the five years since Tristan's death, he'd been feeling like he was drifting, lost. Mariah's presence in his life had become the only constant he could depend on, his only source of actual comfort. Having lost Tristan, he had also lost the one person he'd felt closest to for as far back in life as he could remember. With all of his friends together again, separated from the immediacy of the tragedy that had tainted their last gathering, he was feeling whole and complete in a way he hadn't for so long.

This whole thing had been good for him, and he suspects it's been good for all of them to come together without the specter of Tristan's suicide looming over them like before. In a strange way, to Hewitt, it feels like their friend is still there with them, and maybe he always will be when they are together.

Gale is feeling relaxed as well, so much of his life over the previous years consumed by his work, even here in the place he thought of as being his mountain retreat. Here he is, surrounded by the people closest to him and bringing them into his life in a way he never had before. He'd been wanting to dispense with the compartmentalization between work and the limited personal life he barely even had, and here he was doing precisely that.

He's proud of himself for what he's managed to do in bringing them all together in this secluded place where he hopes they can all get in touch with who they are at the core. Gale sees this as an opportunity to accomplish, for real, the sort of transformation promised by self-help seminars and corporate retreats. This, he believes, will be a real life-changing experience for all of them.

Mariah looks around the table at her friends gathered together, a smile is plastered to her face and her cheeks burn from laughter. It's a shame, she thinks to herself, that they're so rarely able to get together like this. She glances at Hewitt from the corner of her eye and smiles wider, seeing how jovial and unreserved he seems. As happy and content as she knows he is during the time they spend together, just the two of them, this is something different and he looks healthier.

She can only imagine how different she looks compared to her everyday life if this vacation is having such a profound effect on the man she loves. The cheer and pleasure on all the other faces around her must be reflected in her own features, and she is almost overwhelmingly grateful to Gale for bringing them all together like this.

The whole evening is a dizzying whirl for Miles. So much of his life has been spent separate from the civilian world and not much less has been spent outside of the US and a fair amount of that has been squandered in hostile territory. There was plenty of downtime and drinking through the years he spent in the Marine Corps, but Kateb was the only one of his childhood friends present for any of that, and even he wasn't always in the same regions at the same time. This is different, and it is deeply refreshing, in its way, to relax with people where there is no consideration of judgment unless he counts the small group of locals who have been glaring over at them on and off the whole time they've been at the bar.

He thinks the waitress clearly isn't accustomed to larger groups being present either, since she's spending so much of the evening casting side-eyes when she thinks no one is looking.

Of course, he thinks, this is Idaho, and maybe she's just not fond of black and brown folks. It wouldn't be the first time he's fallen outside of someone's preferred color palette. At least he hasn't overheard anyone muttering, "nigger," under their breath, and he probably would have ignored it even if he had. No sense in letting anyone's ignorance ruin what should be a good time.

Kateb has been picking up on the same tension and undercurrent of hostility and he likewise ascribes it to the same shit he'd dealt with all his life; whether it was the darker skin, the obvious Middle Eastern descent, or the less obvious sexuality, he'd learned to cope with biases and negativity long before. Coping with it typically meant brushing it off and partitioning it away to the back of his mind and moving on with his life, precisely what he was doing now.

Besides, there was no sense in letting it bother him. Strangers wouldn't know it, but he's hardly devout in his faith. Most people, he discovered, don't know enough about Islam to know that he shouldn't be drinking. It could be that he likes drinking a little too much. Being surrounded by friends as he presently is, he's certainly intent on enjoying himself. It's traditionally just been himself and Miles hanging out like this, and the additional company is something he considers to be worth celebrating.

Too much drinking has always made him want to smoke, and he was the last of his friends still doing so. Miles had never been a smoker and is always the first to give him shit over the habit, comparing kissing him to the process of licking clean an ashtray, which hardly seems accurate or fair.

Since Tristan's funeral, both Hewitt and Mariah had quit the habit, leaving him as the last holdout with respect to the vice they'd all picked up as teens.

As he stands unsteadily and excuses himself to step outside for a cigarette, he receives the expected taunting and mockery from everyone at the table, the former smokers and the child somehow managing to be the most relentless in haranguing him.

"I've made it two full hours," he replies with mock indignation. "Two hours of you insufferable people, and I am going to smoke before I strangle one of you. Of course, any of you are welcome to join me, you know, aside from the boy."

Laughing, Kateb dramatically spins, almost losing his footing, having overestimated his coordination, and makes his way to the door.

Miles considers joining him outside, not for a cigarette but the company, but decides that he should take advantage of seeing the others while he has the chance to do so. He'll be seeing plenty of Kateb after the vacation has ended.

16

— · —

CHAPTER SIXTEEN

KATEB WAS BORN TO Pakistani immigrants, a father who came to America on a work VISA as an engineer and a mother who, though she hadn't worked in Pakistan, soon established herself as a seamstress with a fantastic eye for detail. Both of them Shia Muslims, they looked to America as a place to escape the everyday persecution and casual bigotry that came from the Sunni majority in their home country during the 1970s.

By the time Kateb was old enough to learn anything about his parents' faith, they had both largely adopted a more secular perspective and practiced their religion more out of tradition and familiarity than any deeply rooted devotion to Islam. The personal God of American Christianity had influenced their faith in dramatic ways.

Kateb benefitted from growing up in a household with both great respect for history and tradition and the flexibility and openness of a normal American family. His parents balanced those two things better than most. The bilingual upbringing instilled a love of language in him at an early age that followed him through the rest of his life.

During his childhood, and especially into his teen years, he often enjoyed teasing his friends about his superior grasp of the English language, even though he'd been raised by immigrants who spoke it exclusively as a second language. It was always good-natured and never spiteful or cruel.

Kateb didn't seem to have a cruel bone in his body, a perspective shared by everyone who knew him. His parents, teachers, and friends always knew he was sensitive in nature and empathetic. Some of these people suspected, well before he realized it for himself, that Kateb was gay. He was already in high school before he came to terms with his sexual orientation and he spent a long time dreading coming out to his parents, his perception of Islamic families being influenced by American media and what he'd seen of bigotry from plenty of the mainstream Christians out there.

He'd had no cause to worry, though. His parents had suspected as much for a long time and had numerous times discussed their son's preferences, just waiting until he was comfortable sharing that part of his life with them.

He never doubted how lucky he was to have the support system he had and the inclusive family he was raised by. Miles, as the friend closest to him and the person he confided in the most, hadn't been so lucky where his father was concerned, which surely contributed to Miles' intense desire to leave him and not look back once high school graduation was out of the way.

Because of the bond they shared, Kateb followed Miles into a life of military service, and his specific bilingual upbringing and cultural heritage guaranteed his value overseas. He learned additional Arabic dialects and was invaluable as an interpreter.

Serendipity combined with some careful planning led to Miles and Kateb running into one another frequently during their respective deployments, but Kateb left the service for college after his four years were up, studying journalism and mass communication, something his friends teased him about as being a dead or at least dying field. He took the mockery in stride and excelled in his courses.

With no interest in pursuing anything beyond a Bachelor's, he struggled to find a place for himself in a field that was indeed dwindling.

Local papers and small market network affiliates gave him some experience, but no sense of fulfillment and it was still a struggle to find decent work in the Midwest, where most of the opportunities for someone fresh out of school could be found. He wasn't sure where to go, but he knew that dead-end reporting and copywriting wasn't it.

It was only after he and Miles spent a weekend together in Las Vegas that he found his calling. Hashing things out with Miles, he began reaching out to his connections within the Corps and within the DOD, obtaining approvals and background clearances necessary to get himself embedded within infantry groups and patrol units.

His reports to the AP needed to go through review and redaction, but he was more than familiar enough with the red tape that he saved someone in the Pentagon some work. The money was nothing to write home about, but the experience felt far more rewarding than anything else he'd done since graduation.

Kateb continued with his work alongside the troops until shortly after Miles' injury, deciding it was time for him to take a break of his own while his friend convalesced. Watching Miles chomping at the bit and fighting to remain a Marine was heart-wrenching for Kateb, knowing he couldn't do a damn thing, though he tried to pull every string he could imagine.

It was during this unexpected downtime when he began tossing around the idea of putting some of his experiences together in a book. Dick Marcinko had made a decent career out of embellished and adequately tweaked versions of his exploits within the Navy, and Kateb certainly believed he was a better writer than whoever had ghostwritten those books.

Six months it took him to compile and revise articles he'd written and to supplement them with suitably altered details he'd left out. The manuscript changed hands via numerous friends and acquaintances within the media and Kateb had a contract not long after.

The next year, his first novel was published. There were no bestseller list breakthroughs or guest invites for Ellen or Oprah, but he was successful enough that the publisher advanced him on a follow-up, and he was able to live more comfortably than he had while he'd been working his way up to that point.

The second book did better than the first, and within certain circles, he was considered quite a success. He toured military bases both in the US and overseas, signing copies of his books for troops who appreciated the way he managed to portray their lives in a way that made them seem noble for their sacrifices and human for the way they still tried to live their lives in conditions that were sometimes virtually unbelievable. He tried to remain stoic while in front of the troops, but all too often he found himself shedding a tear as he found cause to look away for just a moment.

His third book, and the one his agent believed might hit the bestseller list, was about time he'd spent out of the service and the things he'd witnessed while following private military contract escorts in both military and civilian environments overseas. He knew he would be rubbing some people the wrong way and making some enemies in the process, Miles might even be one of them, but he was playing the story close to his chest until he got it finished and finally heard back from his editor.

He left for vacation, expecting to hear back from his editor any day, keeping his phone off during the time away from the world to avoid needing to have a conversation he didn't relish having with Miles.

17

CHAPTER SEVENTEEN

OF COURSE, IT'S STILL raining outside, but the overhang at the entrance of the bar provides shelter enough that Kateb manages not to ruin his cigarette in the process of extracting it from the pack and lighting it. Inhaling that first bitter breath filled with smoke, Kateb sighs. It's the taste he doesn't want to give up.

He's tried vaporizers, nicotine gum, and other smoking alternatives, and they simply did nothing for him. It was that taste of the actual smoke that he loved so much about the habit. If he could find an alternative with the same satisfying flavor, he would have quit long before now. But instead, here he stands, barely sheltered from the rain, breathing in smoke and smiling uncontrollably because the last few days have been a whirlwind of happy memories and nostalgia shared with excellent company.

The stresses and strains of impending middle age, of schedules and deadlines, have been shed temporarily, and he feels like a kid again. He, like most adults, had forgotten how free and comfortable life was when he was younger. As a child, everything had seemed so important and per-manent, but there was so much freedom and so few de-mands compared to life in the real world. It was a part of his life he could never truly get back, but this vacation with his friends was feeling pretty close to providing just that.

Being surrounded by his best friends is making Kateb happier and more content than he's been in a long time. So lost in reverie and the cloudy haze produced by the alcohol, he only marginally takes notice of the couple standing in the alcove almost directly across from him. With his limited attention being mostly focused internally, he suspects they are doing the same thing he is and that they're simply trying to stay relatively dry. He pays it no more mind.

Had he been less distracted, he might have noticed the way they didn't stop staring at him for even a second. Across the distance and through the rain, he might even be able to pick out the twisted expressions on their two faces, an almost familiar combination of fear and contempt. Like Miles, he would probably chalk that up to latent racism and an overall lack of familiarity with non-whites as a whole. Certain things had gotten better over the years, but being associated with Islam hadn't made life particularly easy since the towers fell and the war that never ends had kicked off all those years back. If he did notice them, he would have written them off as harmless, small-town bigots, but he didn't even notice them enough to reach that conclusion.

Kateb does pay some mind to the drunk woman staggering and stumbling his direction along the sidewalk to his right. He is almost finished with the cigarette and is preparing to go back inside to the warmth and camaraderie. She has clearly had more to drink than he has, which says a bit, he thinks to himself as she gets closer. The single-minded focus of her gaze makes him suspect that she's heading his way to ask him for a cigarette. It's familiar bar territory he's navigated countless times, and he's happy to share in most cases, this occasion being no different.

He taps out a new cigarette from the pack and extends it toward the woman as she comes within only a few feet of him. With his left hand, he begins fishing around in his pocket for the lighter he knows is there. He is looking down at his jacket, in search of the elusive lighter, and doesn't see the vacant, hungry look in her eyes or the blood that hasn't fully been rinsed away from her lips and teeth by the rain.

Kateb doesn't know he's being attacked until it happens. The woman's claw-like hands take hold of his outstretched arm, pulling him roughly toward her and crushing his mostly finished cigarette between their bodies. In the time it takes for him to wonder what's happening her teeth have already torn through his jacket and gouged their way into the flesh of his right arm.

The broken cigarette falls from his hand to the sidewalk, and he simultaneously jerks away his injured arm and shoves with his left hand pressed hard against the woman's forehead. Her jaws remain locked in place and a mouthful of flesh, muscle, and fabric goes with her as he violently drives her away. She falls to the sidewalk without even trying to catch herself, still chewing vigorously as she raises herself from the ground, her lunatic eyes still focused on Kateb.

The pain that flares through his nerves at the location of the bite is worse than anything he's felt before. He stumbles away from the woman, picking herself up from the awning-covered sidewalk, hardly willing to accept that he just hit her or that he was forced into that action by the sheer animalistic manner with which she had assaulted him. She didn't even seem human, he tells himself; hoping to relieve some of the guilt over what he's just done, desperately wishing to reconcile the facts within him, to rationalize and perhaps justify what happened. He has no way of knowing how badly he might have injured her, nor how much of the blood on the ground might be hers and how much is his own.

The wound needs to be disinfected. His mind is clear enough to recognize the importance of the fact that no matter how shocked and confused he is, there's no telling just what sort of bacteria might have been colonizing in the madwoman's saliva. From where she hit the ground, now in a seated position, she begins to pull herself up the rest of the way, her movements jerking and peculiar enough to maintain his attention even while he bleeds profusely from his wound.

Confused and in pain, he presses his hand against the wound, applying as much pressure as he can manage. He turns and stumbles his way to the door, hoping to get back into what he thinks of as the safety of the bar interior, wanting to put some distance and obstacles between himself and the crazy woman who'd just bit him.

He clumsily forces his way through the door of the bar, back inside to where his friends are still chatting away, shouldering into it with his good arm. It takes a moment for his friends to notice that something is wrong, but almost as one they register the blood and his unsteady movements. He has no idea that the deranged woman has managed to follow him inside until the looks of shock in his friends' eyes turn to horror and by the time he registers the change, it's far too late. He feels the weight of her dragging him backward, fingers hooked like claws and tugging at him.

Her mouth meets his throat, and the teeth force their way through the resistance of his skin after only a moment. He struggles to push her away with all the force he can manage and when she finally draws away; she takes a mouthful of flesh and muscle with her, sinew snapping as it's yanked past the breaking point. In some place at the back of Kateb's mind, he hears the tearing as it happens and knows that the damage is horrible.

The next thing he's aware of is Miles leaping forward with his thick pint glass in the process of being swung. For a moment, he worries that Miles is planning to attack him, too. Miles connects with all of his force and the glass hits the woman in the left temple hard enough to whip her head back, but the glass doesn't break. He can't tell, but he almost suspects that her neck may have.

As Kateb slips to the floor, Miles attempting to help him down gently. All around is chaos and screaming. His friends rush to where Miles and Kateb are on the floor while everyone else in the bar simply stares without any perceptible reaction.

18

— . —

Chapter Eighteen

Darkness.

All is black, followed seconds later by the unpromising orange light cast by the backup system. The grid had finally taken enough abuse, and a transformer went down. The emergency services building is quiet enough that all Deputy Weber can hear is the rain and sporadic thunder.

He'd sent his solitary prisoner home earlier in the day. The man had calmed down finally, and he'd seemed confused and may not have been feeling well. He figured it was better to have sent the guy home than keep him locked up overnight.

If power is out here, he figures, it's out all over town. Some homes and businesses had generators installed, but judging by the severity of the storm, they are likely to be out of fuel by the time the power can be restored. That leaves only the intermittent lights throughout the downtown area and the medical clinic as still being in the same semi-powered state as the emergency services building, drawing power from the backup system that had never gotten established with the whole town.

It had been in the works for years. There had always been talk of getting the backup lines upgraded to handle the larger draw and replacing the vulnerable lines that followed the road into town, but funding never seemed to be there. Things were going to be interesting, for sure. This is precisely the sort of scenario that leads to panic if it isn't addressed quickly.

No escape with no relief on the horizon, no phones or connections to the outside world, and now there is no power. He figures it's going to be up to him to smooth things out. Thank goodness for a full tank of gas and plenty of reserves. He was going to be doing a great deal of driving over the next however many days, delivering fuel where needed to keep generators running and helping people if homes began to flood. Besides, he knows, sometimes it takes no more than the presence of an authority figure to diffuse tension in situations like these.

"There'll be no rest for me now," he mutters to himself, chuckling as he gears up to head back out into the torrent. The cruiser SUV and its flashing lights will be a beacon, he figures. The sort of thing people will be looking to for stability in stressful moments. He's the closest there is to someone being in charge.

19

— · —

Chapter Nineteen

Kateb has hardly stopped breathing before the lights go out. The bar has an old gas generator, but it isn't quick to start and in those seconds an eternity seems to pass and the darkness lends itself to the confusion and panic the friends are experiencing.

The only light slips through the windows from the small number of streetlights connected to an emergency power backup. In an area with routine blizzards throughout the winter, those sorts of preparations have saved countless lives in the years since they were added. Right now, those lights illuminate the panic and terror in the eyes of Kateb's friends, and the tears freely streaming from Miles' eyes as he watches his closest friend leave him behind.

The handful of patrons who had watched the attack with passive indifference slowly make their way outside, casually ignoring the horror. The waitress who had seemed to be giving them a bit of a cold shoulder the whole evening, glares at them where they are huddled around Kateb for the next minute before lunging at them, frenzied. Mariah is the closest to the waitress, her back turned to the assault, but Miles catches the movement from the corner of his eye and reacts before anyone else even has time to process what's happening.

From where he'd been squatting on the floor, he drops to a knee and his size-15 boot on the free foot connects with the waitress where her abdomen meets her chest. There is an audible crack from the xiphoid process—and hopefully some ribs—that can be heard over the thump of the contact itself. The woman flies back and the middle of her spine hits a nearby table with enough force to send it sliding another foot in the direction the woman was traveling when she made impact. She slumps to the floor, unconscious and quite possibly injured enough to be dying.

Miles doesn't care one way or another. He takes a moment to think about what he's just done and realizes he feels nothing at all. There is only fury and despair, no room for anything else at the moment. He looks back down to where Kateb lies on the floor right in front of him, bleeding out on the floor of a dive bar in the middle of some nowhere town.

The two of them had been through experiences that most people couldn't imagine, in places that they often joked would make Hell seem favorable. They had been as close as two people could ever hope to be, as close as Miles could imagine being with anyone.

"God damn!" Hewitt finally says, the first actual words spoken by any of their group since Kateb had stumbled through the door.

"Thank you," Mariah says, only realizing the danger she'd been in after Miles had taken care of it.

Abraham glances out the window and can make out people standing out there, shuffling around in the rain, their furtive movements visible to him in the light cast by the streetlights. From where he's positioned, they appear to be expectantly watching the front of the bar.

He's sure that they can't see inside, through the limited light available and the gaps in the advertisements on the windows are few and far between. The way they are congregating and talking to each other, heedless of the rain and fixated on the door of the bar, begins to make him exceptionally uncomfortable. Something is going on that he doesn't understand, that he's sure none of them do.

Ben sits petrified in the chair where he remained through everything that happened, and his father is grateful to know that he was on the opposite side of the group from where the waitress had attacked them.

"We need to start thinking about getting the hell out of here," Abraham says, gesturing outside. The others look up at him and their eyes follow the way he's pointing.

A chill travels down Hewitt's spine as he watches the strangers waiting for them outside. That's precisely what they're doing. He knows it without any question, waiting for them to step outside. What comes next, he has no idea, but he doesn't relish the thought of discovering their intentions. While the group peers through the windows, another couple of locals show up, making a total of seven people standing around out there, and the odds are things just going to get worse.

The evening that had started so relaxed and jovial was steadily transforming into a nightmare. It takes them a few more seconds to notice that the tires are flat on Gale's van, which is parked right there next to the curb. They all seem to notice this fact at the same time, and they all assume that the same will be true for Abraham's truck, which is parked just a little farther down the block.

Zombie attacks, hostile small-town waitresses, all following a storm that knocked out transportation, communication, and now the majority of the power.

"What the fuck is going on here?" Hewitt asks out loud, directed less at his friends than at the universe itself.

"Miles," Gale says calmly, "we need to leave Kateb here and get away from this place quickly."

Miles shakes his head, tears in his eyes, not disagreeing with his friend's suggestion, but unable to imagine leaving him there on that floor.

"It's ok," Mariah says as she gently touches his shoulder. "He would want you to get out of here, too. You know he would."

Hewitt glances out the window. No one has come any closer to the bar. "We're heading back to your place, Gale. And then we are finding some way out of this fucked up little town."

There are no new arrivals outdoors, but each of them knows that this won't remain the case. The friends all find their way to their feet, Abraham nudging Ben to stand as well.

As they approach the door, Gale turns, "We should probably split up and spread them out a bit."

"As much as I hate that you just went there," Hewitt replies, "I have to agree."

They quickly pair off with one another; Mariah and Gale together, Abraham and Ben sticking with one another, leaving Miles and Hewitt to go their own way. They inhale deeply, trying to calm their nerves before they open the door and bolt. None of the strangers immediately take off after Mariah and Gale. A couple begin racing after Abraham and Ben, but the five of the remaining number follow Miles and Hewitt.

"It's because I'm black, isn't it?" Miles shouts back over his shoulder, managing to joke, and he sprints off into the dark space between the intermittent streetlamps. Hewitt's too focused on his speed and avoiding tripping over anything to laugh, but he appreciates the humor just the same.

Risking a quick look back, Hewitt feels his amusement immediately fade and his stomach churn. Two of the five pursuers are noticeably closer and gain ground quickly. An old joke comes to mind, and he thinks, *Miles doesn't need to run faster than the townsfolk. He just needs to run faster than me.*

"We're going to need to split up too, I think," Hewitt spits out breathlessly after weighing the odds.

Miles grunts in affirmation as he takes a quick look behind them as well.

"At the corner," he says.

The two of them pick up their speed, sprinting as fast as they can, and as they reach the corner, they each turn down the cross street in opposite directions. The townsfolk split off to follow them after a brief moment conferring amongst themselves, three of them continuing to chase Miles and the other two resuming their pursuit of Hewitt. Both of them hope the delay while the locals decide what to do will be enough to give them a chance, but neither of them is optimistic.

20

Chapter Twenty

Terror is the only reasonable response to what is happening. Terror is what Miles is experiencing now, overshadowing even the devastating sense of loss.

Even his experiences on the battlefield are insufficient to insulate Miles from the sheer horror he feels as he races down the darkened streets, dodging from one pool of shadow to the next. Combat never came as a surprise when he was deployed to one hell hole or another, as much as he and his brothers and sisters might try to relax and occasionally let loose, they always knew where they were and that hostile territory could, at any time, present hostile situations. This was something else entirely. Being attacked and hunted in some small American town felt like something his grandfather or great-grandfather would have dealt with, but nothing he should have been prepared for.

If this is something racially motivated, it is far and above anything he had ever prepared himself for. He's lost the men who were following him after he and Hewitt separated, but they can't be too far behind. Dodging into an empty yard and cutting through a dark alley seemed like a good idea when he'd done it, but he now begins to question the wisdom of avoiding his immediate threat by opening himself up to far more unknowns. A noise ahead of him sets his nerves on edge and he slips further off the center of the alley and into what appears to be an empty backyard.

The lack of light penetrating through the windows is fucking meaningless, the only operational electricity seeming to be dedicated to the occasional streetlamp. Something seems off about that, he muses, but there's nothing he can do about it now. The back door is locked, and he doesn't want to risk drawing any attention to himself by breaking the glass or attempting to bust the door down. Through the window, he sees nothing, no signs of movement, but he can't make out much detail and doesn't trust that he's seeing everything he might need to see.

He creeps along the side of the house, a tight squeeze between the home and the fence separating the adjoining property from this one. More noise from behind him, back in the alley, but he doesn't look back. The front of the house will leave him exposed, nothing but a stereotypical picket fence along the sidewalk, but there's no movement he can see, and the house is mostly sheltered from the closest streetlight nearly half a block away.

Silently, he rushes up the steps as fast as he can without making a ruckus of it. The door handle turns easily in his hands, and he pushes the door open, wary that there could be anything waiting for him in the dark interior. He pulls the door closed again and slips along the wall to the right, trying to avoid standing out in silhouette at all.

Miles crosses the dark living room, his movements slow and deliberate. The house appeared empty as he crossed the backyard and peered through the first-floor windows that faced the alley, but that was no guarantee that the occupants weren't present. The door had been unlocked, which meant that there was a good chance he wouldn't be alone inside, and he had let himself in with all the stealth that he could manage, conscious of just how much risk he was taking.

He stands silently in the entryway between the kitchen and living space for close to five minutes, listening to the silence of the place, attuned to the slightest whisper of his breathing until the sound of his pulse in his ear's echoes like a drum. He doesn't make the slightest motion until he assures himself that nothing moves in the almost pitch-black interior of the residence.

His foot descends softly and the faintest creak of the floorboard beneath causes him to immediately shift his full weight back to the other. His breath halts mid-exhale and his eyes widen as he scans his surroundings with sweeping movements of his eyes; counting on his peripheral vision to catch anything that might pose a threat, his head remains, like the rest of his body, as still as a living statue, each muscle tensed to react at the slightest impetus.

Even within the deathly silent structure, he is aware that the noise couldn't have been a fraction of the volume that it was to him, but he is unwilling to risk the possibility of being discovered by anyone that might be there. There was no chance of the sound carrying beyond the walls, but still, Miles worries that his misstep could draw the attention of either of the threats currently roaming the town. The tension and heightened state of fear are making him paranoid, he knows. He's seen it countless times in war zones, but he's seen that same paranoia save plenty of lives, including his own.

The kitchen holds little of value, though he grabs a butcher knife from the block on the counter, feeling better just having something he can use to defend himself as he searches the rest of the house. In the den, he discovers something that makes him want to cry tears of gratitude. Above the mantle is an older, over-under shotgun. It wouldn't have been his choice of firearm, but under the circumstances, it feels like a miracle being bestowed upon him. He moves as quickly as he can without risking tripping over something and slides the gun from the hooks that held it in place.

For a moment, Miles's face displays a sense of awe and gratitude, like he was receiving communion. In a chest to the left of the fireplace, he finds the box of shells; birdshot is not what he would have preferred, but it's better than nothing at all. He breaks the gun open and loads two shells.

Slowly and carefully, Miles explores the ground level of the house, checking every door, including those of pantries and cupboards. It's difficult without any light source to aid him in his search, but his eyes have adjusted enough that he doesn't want to risk destroying his night vision by using the flashlight feature on his phone or the small LED attached to his keychain.

In the den again, he severs the leg of a table as quietly as possible, wanting to be sure that there's something other than the shotgun to rely on in a pinch and something with better reach than the knife he's still carrying. The ground floor is clear, and it's time to head upstairs.

The second stair from the top creaks beneath his weight and he stops dead, slowing his breathing to listen to the noise of the house itself. The rain should have masked the sound, he hopes, but it would similarly mask any other noises he might need to hear. The landing of the second floor leads off to a single door to his right and a hall to his left with two more doors in that direction, all of them closed.

The room to his right is a simple bathroom, white tile floors aiding him in seeing that there's no one inside. The first door along the hall opens on a bedroom that appears to be a child's room, as empty as the rest of the house. The second door along the hall is open already, and he silently slips through and into what must be the master bedroom. He can't quite see the far edges of the room, but he feels the space around him open up.

There is a sudden noise to his right and Miles turns that direction, his feet sliding as he pivots. In the darkness, something latches onto him with hands clawing at him like a hungry animal, clutching at him and struggling to pull him towards it, or itself towards him. Either way, it amounts to the same thing.

The shotgun in Miles' hands erupts with an almost deafening explosion that immediately sets his ears ringing and the hands are no longer there holding onto him. Something wet and substantial hits the ground a few feet from where he stands. Almost immediately he begins walking backward slowly towards the open doorway that he knows is there, and he can hear the hungry thing in the darkness shifting itself around, breath gurgling in its throat. He can't be sure where he hit it with the shot, but the damage has to be massive at that proximity.

It drags itself across the floor, slipping out of the deeper shadows of the bedroom, the gender that it might have been before disguised by the severity of its wound. Still, it moves inexorably forward, hauling itself forward with single-minded focus, desperate to reach its prey even as the final traces of life begin to dissipate within it. There is no question that its momentum should have ceased sometime before; everything he can make out in the darkness tells him this person should be dead, but somehow it just keeps dragging itself along, leaving a trail of blood punctuated by viscera at irregular intervals.

Miles is grateful that he can't make out greater detail in the darkness and that the blast from the shotgun had temporarily impacted his night vision. Miles had seen some terrible things in combat, been party himself to some of the most monstrous actions that one human being can perform against another, but in the minute or so that he has spent watching this creature crawl its way towards him in the half-light, he feels bile surging against his esophagus. Worse than the appearance; the hoarse, guttural groan that issues from its ravaged throat forces Miles' teeth to clench.

Finally, Miles raises the table leg, wielding it like a sledge-hammer, and brings it crashing down onto the ghoul's skull, again and again until he can no longer distinguish be-tween the sounds of splintering wood and bone. So much more silent than the shotgun that had initially shredded its body had been. The noise is still so much worse. He finally takes a moment to mutter a prayer to any gods that might be listening that the sound of gunfire somehow hadn't managed to attract the attention of others like the thing he had just dispatched, perhaps within the same house.

"This simply cannot be happening," Miles whispers to himself as he begins to analyze what he can remember of the town's layout, working out the best route available to him back to Gale's home and the SUV that he left parked there.

Everyone would be making their way there as well, any-one still alive at least. But the rest of them don't all know about the firearms and ammunition that Miles carries in a false compartment in the back of every vehicle he's owned, so he muses hopefully that Gale is armed, or he makes it back there quickly enough for it to make a difference. It seems that his obsessive preparations for terrible scenarios has finally proven itself to be not only worthwhile but imperative.

He drops the splintered table leg, casting it aside with disgust. Miles heads downstairs and slips back through the front door, not knowing if the kitchen exit will be safe and almost certain that the noise of the shotgun had gotten the attention of whatever had been moving around in the alley behind the house.

21

CHAPTER TWENTY-ONE

Finally having lost the crazy locals who were hunting him, catching his breath and his bearings next to a dumpster, Hewitt realizes he drew the short-end of the stick when he and Miles had diverged to make a more difficult target for the assholes. He is heading in the opposite direction of Gale's house, and he can't be certain just how far out of the way he's gotten or how difficult it's going to be to get back on track.

Tucked against the wall of the building, hidden in the shadow provided by the dumpster, he's heard multiple groups of people passing by and it's only a matter of time before one of these gangs head down the alley where he will be an easy target. This place is turning out to be far from the restful vacation spot he imagined when they were at the lake just the day before.

He has no idea what is going on around him, but Hewitt knows that he and his friends are somehow the targets of some crazy doomsday cult or something equally unlikely. He does his best not to think about the fact that Kateb had been killed by a goddamn zombie, or someone so strung out and sick that they may as well have been one. He shifts his focus to other things, only to have momentary flashes of what happened in the bar force their way to the forefront of his mind, whether he likes it or not.

The scared, desperate look on Kateb's face as Miles struggled to apply pressure to the ragged, gushing wound isn't something he thinks he'll ever forget. They'd come here to commemorate the anniversary of one lost friend, and now there was one more death—at least one more death—added to the epitaph of their childhood. He shakes his head in frustration, trying to think his way out of this, desperate to find a sensible solution to something that thus far hasn't made a bit of sense.

First things first, he needs to find better shelter than this wet alley. The smell of garbage piled up only feet away from him is rekindling his desire to vomit. He dodges his way through the shadows, feeling at least a little lucky that the power appears to be out throughout the town, aside from the occasional streetlights that must have been storing solar power before the storm hit.

His chance of making it to Gale's house plummets as he reaches the end of the alley. The street is teeming with a crowd of local people waving flashlights and shouting, and they're all clustered in the direction he needs to go. The opposite direction seems clear, but there's less light that direction which could be a good thing or the worst thing possible. He considers returning to the street from which he'd entered the alley, wondering if maybe it'll be clearer that way, but as he glances behind him he sees silhouettes moving down the path, silent as ghosts.

His decision made for him, Hewitt slips out of the alley, hugging the wall as if his life depends on it, which it very well might, and when he's confident that he's made it to deeper darkness, he begins to run. Of course, he's running further away from his destination, but going the wrong way and staying alive is better than going the really wrong way and winding up very much dead.

He only has to avoid a couple of smaller parties, presumably hunting for him. He finally makes it to a more residential neighborhood on the far side of town. Which is, by far, more disturbing than the residents who were actively hunting for him.

Ducking into a tool shed that was thankfully left accessible with a padlock that hadn't been engaged, Hewitt is out of the rain for a minute and can catch his breath. He's more exhausted than he could have anticipated from the constant stops and starts as he evaded patrols and made his way to this relative safety.

The town has become something sinister. The quaint, small-town environment feels like it's closing in around him as Hewitt peers out from his hiding place in the shed through sheets of pouring rain.

Shelter was hard to find, but at least he's tucked away from the worst of the precipitation where no one is going to see him without actively searching for him. He can finally relax for a bit and attempt to find some way to backtrack where he needs to be going. It probably won't afford him enough time to analyze what had happened, but it was going to be better than nothing.

He worries that he might have experienced some sort of massive disconnect from the real world and those fears only get worse the more he attempts to analyze the events in the bar. The woman who attacked Kateb had appeared to be a zombie, something right out of the movies they'd all watched since they were children. His earlier thoughts that she might be a junkie were nothing more than a transparent attempt to rationalize the irrational. That is where this nightmare had started. But the more he thinks about things, he recalls a strange sort of tension from the locals even before that event had taken place. There was a tension even back when they'd been in the diner only a couple of days before.

At the time, Hewitt dismissed it as being more of an internal problem with his perspective. He felt like they were outsiders because they were, and he had always been sort of sensitive about that kind of thing. He'd always been more sensitive than it made sense to be about a lot of things. An off-hand remark from Miles had led him to suspect that it might be less a matter of his perspective than something to do with the demographics of the region and a whole lot to do with an undercurrent of unrepentant racism.

Looking back now, it all becomes more ominous and foreboding. After the unexpected and fatal assault, the casual, cruel indifference of both staff and patrons at the bar had been almost as horrifying as the attack itself. His friend was bleeding profusely from the tear in his throat and the relatively minor wound on his arm, but the only people who seemed to be interested were his friends.

The other people in the bar didn't even seem to care much about the local woman who'd been killed right in front of them after she'd attacked Kateb. It was obvious, in retrospect, that there was something wrong with these people; but Hewitt and his friends had more pressing matters to worry about at the time. Miles had tried his hardest to stop the bleeding, but Kateb was too far gone. Even with medical care immediately available, it would have done no good.

The desperate escape from the bar and the locals who'd been lurking outside in wait seems like a blur. The whole damn thing seems like a senseless, feverish blur. They'd separated, just like idiots always seem to when these types of scenarios play out in movies, which Hewitt now suspects might not have been the brightest idea; but the locals had become hostile towards them in a way that transcended scowls and unpleasant looks.

Whether it is indicative of burgeoning insanity from being pushed beyond what he's prepared to cope with or simply a terribly off-color sense of humor, Hewitt has what he considers to be a great idea. His iPod is still in his pocket and he fishes it out, connecting the earbuds and placing the left in his ear, leaving the right dangling so that he will still be able to hear anyone that might be sneaking up on him.

It only takes him a few seconds of scrolling through the music library to find what he was looking for, and there it is, the perfect song for the occasion. As *Escape From Hellview* begins playing, he grabs a hammer and a small camping hatchet from the shelves within the shed, ventures carefully out of the temporary shelter, and slowly jogs through the darkened streets. Through the downpour, he darts from shadow to shadow.

The town seems empty, but he knows that is an illusion. There is danger everywhere around him and one misstep is all it will take to bring that danger down on him in a bad way. He has to find his way back to Gale's house.

First, he has to find a more secure shelter and straighten his head out after what had happened to Kateb. His mind keeps circling back to the reality that he has to find his friends again, and Gale's house is where they should all be going; it's the only place he can think of to go under the circumstances. If they aren't there, he has no idea where they could be, but at least it serves as a place to start.

The town can't be more than seven miles from one end to the other, but the relative safety of Gale's house feels a world away in every sense possible. He has no idea what sort of hurdles are going to be blocking his attempt to get back where he hopes he'll find his friends again.

The heavy rain and limited visibility have already made navigating these unfamiliar, narrow streets difficult enough, but he is actively being hunted by not only the lunatics living in this town but the zombies as well, assuming there are more of them. Lacking anything better to call them, that's what they were. Zombies.

It's like being trapped in a nightmare. There's no telling whether Kateb has been the only casualty by this time. For all he knows, he is the last of his friends still breathing and untouched by whatever has tainted the residents; but he can't allow himself to dwell on those thoughts or he might just give up all hope.

22

CHAPTER TWENTY-TWO

ABRAHAM HAS A DIFFICULT time processing what he's seeing, peering down from the attic window through the torrent. Ben sleeps fitfully on a nest of folded blankets off to the right of the dusty aperture. Two larger groups of flashlight and headlamp equipped locals converge on a solitary figure who's run out of places to run. The individual doesn't look familiar to him. Even over the distance and through the windblown sheets of rain buffeting the world outside, Abraham can tell this isn't one of his friends. He has to assume the victim being a stranger, it must be another local.

Whoever this stranger is, they fight like a trapped animal. Clearly, they don't belong to either of the two groups converging on them. The shouting and jeering voices are only occasionally audible between bursts of thunder and the rain pummeling the roof, but it doesn't require much clarity to register the hostility in the distance. These people are a mob and an angry one. Obviously, it isn't just Abraham and his friends being targeted by these assholes, but that isn't a source of comfort once he takes the time to unpack the implications of that detail.

Ben snorts and rouses himself with the sound. He looks around, disoriented for a moment, before catching a glimpse of his father sitting in the shadows near the window.

In a whisper, he asks, "Are we still safe here?"

"So far, so good," Abraham replies. "There's been no noise from downstairs and no one outside has so much as glanced up this way."

Ben eases his way over to sit beside his father, taking in the scene below where the mobs have closed on the figure, still struggling to fight.

"How long will we be safe here?"

"I wish I knew, kiddo," Abraham mutters, his voice sad and defeated. "I don't think we're safe anywhere as long as we stick around this town."

He sighs, watching the violence in the street below for a few seconds before continuing, "We need to get back to Gale's house before we do anything else. That's where the rest of them will be."

The individual being hunted outside has stopped struggling. Unconscious or dead, Abraham supposes it doesn't matter. A couple of the larger men from the mob kneel next to the body on the pavement, doing something he can't make out. It takes a minute before Abraham is finally able to see that they were lashing the victim's wrists and ankles together. After the work of binding the captives is done, one of the men hefts the prisoner over his shoulders in a fireman's carry and the collective moves away down the street, probably in search of more prey.

"Alright, son, now is probably as good a chance as we're going to get," Abraham says as he stands, stretches out the stiffness he hadn't noticed while sitting there for so long, and bundles himself in his jacket.

Ben follows his father's lead and gets himself prepared to return outside. They silently lower the hidden stairs back down from the ceiling of the second-floor hallway and cautiously descend to that position. Abraham carries a camping hatchet he located in a shed a few houses away and Ben holds a wrought iron fireplace poker at the ready, their eyes searching the nearly impenetrable darkness for any hint of movement. The weapons leave a lot to be desired, but they both feel better armed with something than they had earlier in the night.

The house remains still and silent as the two make their creeping progress downstairs and to the front door. Abraham peers outside and sees nothing at ground level he hadn't seen from above.

"We're going to stick to the shadows as well as we can and we're going to follow that crowd at a safe distance. They're going the direction I think we need to be headed."

Ben looks up at his father, confused and frightened.

"They're heading the same direction we are. There's no avoiding it, unless I've totally lost my bearings," Abraham responds to the unspoken question from his son.

They remain in silence a little while before he continues, "Besides, I'd rather have these psychos in front of us than sneaking up from behind."

Ben nods in response after a moment of contemplation and stands ready to venture outside. As Abraham opens the door, the rain pelts their exposed skin like hundreds of tiny bee stings. They dart outside, closing the door behind them.

23

Chapter Twenty-Three

BEAMS FROM FLASHLIGHTS SPORADICALLY break up the otherwise absolute darkness of this residential block between the strobes of lightning. Sweeping through the shadows, these beacons are the only reliable way to discern where the hunting townsfolk happen to be on the prowl. The rainfall is too heavy for footsteps or conversation to be overheard until it is far too late for the warning to make a difference. Mariah and Gale know that the same ambient conditions offer them some degree of comfort. For Mariah, though, attempting to navigate an unfamiliar place with no light source of their own is hellish.

They know the approximate direction they need to travel to get back to Gale's house and the tenuous security that might offer, but avoiding the scattered hunting parties all over town has kept them from making a straight shot of it or allowed them to proceed with anything like good time. Mariah has had to focus on Gale. He was the only one who could direct her safely to the house. Unable to let herself worry about what was going on with the others or whether any of them would be there at Gale's when the two of them finally arrived.

From shadow to shadow, yard to yard, they gradually find themselves in a neighborhood that seems familiar to her and Gale confirms it; houses emerge from the darkness that should be only a block or two from their destination if Mariah recalls correctly in her admittedly rattled state of mind. Gale is scared, as anyone should be, but he doesn't seem to be nearly as frightened as she is.

Mariah is proud of him, but she wonders how much of that stoicism is shock and how much of it might be that her friend simply isn't grasping just how real and mortal the danger happens to be. Gale was never one for survivalism or violence for sport the way most of them were, and this sort of situation could be taking a massive toll on her friend's state of mind.

Slogging through pools of standing water seemingly every few feet, they finally see the massive home looming ahead of them. It is illuminated briefly by a flash of lighting but otherwise residing in impenetrable blackness, sheltered from any traces of light from the occasional streetlights that seem to still be operational. There doesn't appear to be anyone there, but she hopes their friends wouldn't be stupid enough to do anything obvious to announce their presence if they had made it back to the house. More important than the apparent emptiness of the house itself, there doesn't appear to be any of the frenzied mob blocking the path.

"We're going to make a break for it and run from here, buddy," Mariah shouts, leaning in close so that Gale can hear her over the sounds of the storm.

He nods, acknowledging that he heard and that he's prepared to make the run for safety.

"No more sneaking," she continues. "Straight up the center of the road this time."

Again Gale nods and this time tosses her a thumbs up and a crooked smile she can only halfway make out. Another couple of flashes, to imprint the scene as best they can in their minds' eyes, and they bolt from a hedge where they've been sheltering themselves from the worst of the storm's fury. The street is wet, but there isn't the standing water to contend with in the center of the road that they were dealing with in the yards and alleys on the way here.

Mariah moderates her speed to keep Gale slightly ahead of her, and they run as fast as either of them ever has. Almost there. As they approach the half block of undeveloped real estate that separates Gale's property from his nearest neighbor, Mariah happens to catch a trace of movement from the corner of her eye during a momentary burst of light.

Staring out, hungrily, from a giant picture window is a woman who looks indistinguishable from something out of a horror movie, the sort of midnight broadcast with zombies or possession involved. Whatever had been in effect with that stranger who had murdered Kateb, this lady had it worse. She looked inhuman, ravenous. The noise from the storm drowns out everything, but Mariah swears she almost hears the concussions as the trapped woman beats against the glass with her ruined hands, leaving bloody prints all over the interior surface.

There is no doubt that this woman saw them. The banging became noticeably more frantic after Mariah had seen her because they'd seen one another at the same time. It was lunacy. She was clearly ill and suffering from whatever sickness the woman at the diner had been afflicted with. She and Gale needed to keep running, and fast because she had no idea how long those panes of glass would hold, and she didn't want to be anywhere within sight when that crazed bitch came careening through the window.

It seems to take them forever, like in those dreams where the ground seems to give with each step and no matter how hard you push yourself, the speed just isn't there. Finally, they do reach the house and Gale approaches one of his cars in the driveway. He nudges Mariah gently by the shoulder, prompting her to stay where she is.

It takes him only a minute or so to fish his keys from the pocket of his sodden jeans, access the driver's side door, and retrieve a Glock 9mm from under the seat where it's fitted into a holster. He and Mariah slowly make their way to the relative shelter of the overhang at the front door. Gale hands the gun to Mariah while he flips through his keys for the one he needs to get them inside.

Ejecting the magazine to be sure it's full before slapping it back into place, Mariah feels much better. She doesn't even think to question why Gale would have a firearm in his car. The gun might not be much help, under the circumstances they'd encountered so far, but it makes her feel better than being unarmed and exposed. They've regained some semblance of having solid ground beneath their feet. She comforts herself with that small victory. Gale pushes the door open and gestures for her to follow him in. At least they can relax, finally out of the downpour.

24

Chapter Twenty-Four

End Transmission by AFI transitions into *The End* by The Beta Machine as Hewitt continues his repeatedly failed attempt to cut back the direction he knows he's supposed to be going. His end of the world playlist is feeling more and more appropriate each time the locals have his path blocked and he's forced to navigate a new route.

They know he's out here and they seem to have some idea as to where he's trying to go. He could be reading too much into things, but he can't shake the thought that he's all alone out here and that his friends heading to Gale's house are fucked. Two more streets are no-go, filled with locals milling about. This whole process of going street to street, only to be cut off isn't working for him. He needs to think things through and find a better way to go about all of this.

Quickly checking all directions, he only takes a moment to finally look up. Taking a moment to catch his breath as he sorts out his next steps, all he can do is dwell on wondering how they got here, whether there was some way this whole turn of events could have been foreseen.

TRISTAN IS GONE, SWALLOWED by his misery—and before he could experience the apparent zombie apocalypse they'd witnessed in movies and video games for so much of their lives. That's not what's really going on. Hewitt knows that, but it's close enough that he wishes he had his best friend by his side.

He can't even imagine what Miles is going through. He lost something more than his best friend. Kateb is gone, brutally murdered in front of his closest friends, and the man he loved—and who loved him.

THEY HAD COME TOGETHER as children, an unlikely group consisting of individuals who simply didn't fit into any of the other cliques that began to develop as early as those final years of elementary school. They bonded over their inability to connect with the other kids. That bond just kept flourishing as they grew up, growing together rather than apart, as so many childhood friendships seem to go.

Many of the ways they spent their time together were like any other eclectic group of children; hiking through the forest and letting their imaginations run wild, hanging out at the arcade for more hours than any parents would appreciate, or climbing around on playground equipment in ways not recommended by adults.

There were other ways they spent their time that would have probably not been quite so typical, though not necessarily alarming; trespassing in abandoned or condemned buildings, sneaking out at night to explore construction sites and finding ways onto rooftops of apartment buildings and businesses to see if they could navigate their way to neighboring rooftops and new, unexplored places. Everyone appeared so small from so high above. Down below, they were always oblivious.

Crowds of drunken revelers would mill about on the sidewalks below with no idea what was going on above them. There was a definite thrill involved in being able to watch strangers going about their evenings without any knowledge that they were being stalked and monitored by a group of peculiar children. As they got older, the explorations began to lean more heavily toward those latter activities and other things that could have gotten the whole group of them into trouble.

A fascination with horror films and post-apocalyptic movies influenced them heavily, as it does adolescents all around, those of a certain personality type at least. They would meet in the middle of the night at the cemetery near Gale and Mariah's neighborhood, at first just to wander around and soak up the ambiance and to drink and smoke the cigarettes they were too young to be smoking as they progressed further into their teen years.

As they became teenagers, the explorations of off-limit locations began to take on a different quality and they started to refer to it as "post-apocalyptic boot camp." They were kids fascinated by any and all manner of apocalyptic scenarios. Not an uncommon thing in and of itself. Their preferred fantasies, naturally, combined their mutual love of horror with the apocalypse. All of them were avid fans of George A. Romero, Lucio Fulci, and other directors who specialized in zombies overtaking the world of the living.

The kids collected knives, swords, hatchets, and all other things that they thought might prepare them for the most unlikely of futures. Gradually, as they got older, they joined family members on hunting trips and visits to shooting ranges, for the simple fun of it as well as the preparation they felt it would provide if the end happened to come.

For the most part, they were just kids being kids, but there was a darker bent to the way this group of seven friends chose to entertain themselves. Others came and went over the years, joining and leaving the group for a variety of reasons, just the way children naturally come and go in one another's lives. Those seven friends were virtually inseparable.

There were certainly areas where interests diverged. Hewitt, Gale, Mariah, and Tristan became rather fond of role-playing games. It began with D&D and the numerous expansions on that universe but it wasn't long before Shadowrun, Cyberpunk, and Call of Cthulhu became regular parts of the rotation as well.

While the four played their games, Miles, Kateb, and Abraham participated in various athletic activities, either for the school or other organizations. Miles and Kateb both signed up for ROTC as soon as it was an option for them in school. As their lives expanded into different, larger circles, they remained active in one another's lives and never neglected to support each other in their assorted pursuits.

On weekends, Miles and Kateb would often run the others through drills that were variations of what they experienced in ROTC. The whole group was happy to remain active; and though Gale was the first to complain during these strenuous exertions, he was still present for these exhausting activities just the same.

Whenever possible they would study together or work out tutoring schedules to assist anyone that might be falling behind. Through high school graduation, they worked together to ensure that everyone got through it all just fine. Most of the tutoring was done by Tristan and Hewitt, as those two seemed to excel at any subject put in front of them. Gale was superb where science and mathematics were concerned and Mariah was an excellent student of history and the arts; they would both chip in with tutoring duties where their areas of expertise came into play.

Kateb was a good all-around student, but nowhere near the top of the class. Miles only really felt that he was standing out where athletics were concerned, though he also displayed a surprising proficiency in drama. Abraham's skill set didn't appear until he was provided with a wood shop and the ability to work with machines. Working together, though, all seven of them graduated with honors.

They spent a couple of weeks, all of them together, following graduation, before they struck out on their own and went their separate ways. From that autumn forward they tried to keep in touch and get together as best they could manage. Life got in the way a lot of the time, more often than not, for some more than others. Adulthood changed their relationships with one another, but the friendship and connection remained strong.

CREEPING ALONG THE ROOFTOP of a general store he accessed by a ladder in the alley, he catches a glimpse of a familiar and comforting pattern of lights only a couple of blocks away. It may be clutching at straws, but the presence of a police cruiser is at least some potential chance that he isn't alone. He watches long enough to assure himself it's stationary. Assured, and with renewed purpose, he returns to the ladder and scrabbles down to the alley below.

He drops to the alley floor just as another of the zombie things was passing by. He holds his breath and flattens himself against the wall, willing himself to be invisible and hoping that he's been unnoticed. Too late. The noise of his impact drew its attention and as it turns toward him, hungry and rasping, it's inarticulate language impossible to misinterpret, Hewitt freezes for a second.

He's never killed anyone before and though he's not entirely certain this counts, he is having a difficult time accepting what he needs to do. Grasping, desperate hands reach for him and he knows that this is death approaching in the most unlikely form.

He raises the hammer he'd collected from the shed and swings it down with the claw end, impacting the man's forehead just above the left eye with a crunch that immediately makes him feel ill. In the half-light, he imagines he can see splinters of bone jaggedly protruding from the wound. Spurts of blood mimic the rhythm of the stranger's fading heartbeat. The man quickly becomes dead weight, pulling at the hammer in Hewitt's hand, and it slides from his grip as the victim falls to the asphalt of the alley.

He stands there staring at the ground in front of him, fixated on the dead man, hammer still protruding from his vacant face, the rain washing away what little blood there is from the wound. He can't bring himself to extract the hammer from the zombie's skull; leaving it where it's embedded, he backs away the direction of the lights he'd seen. The hatchet will have to be good enough to get him safely there, and he desperately finds himself hoping that he doesn't need to use it.

Just Another Day by Oingo Boingo ends and Hewitt rips out the earbud as Lars Frederiksen's *Army of Zombies* begins playing. What had seemed funny and amusing before just wasn't funny anymore. There's nothing cute about what's happening and what he's just been forced to do has soured what his friends had always considered an indomitable sense of humor and levity. Deep inside, somewhere he rarely ventured, he had always been aware that his ability to find humor in pretty much anything was a mask of some kind or little more than a coping mechanism.

He's becoming conscious of that fact now as despair floods through the cracks in that facade. It's only his focus on finding someone in some tenuous position of authority that pushes him onward from the site of the murder he's just committed.

PROGRESS IS SLOW AS Hewitt exercises greater caution, hoping to avoid any surprises like he'd experienced coming down from the rooftop. There are more of the zombies and more gangs of local assholes roaming about, but they're clearly not on the same side, as Hewitt discovers as he watches three men in an offshoot of the mob swarmed by five of the unthinking eaters. The sight is awful, but strangely, not quite as bad as some of the things he's seen in movies.

He recognizes that distance, and no small amount of shock is playing a role in his being so detached, and he moves on. He continues with his mission, knowing that no one in the immediate vicinity is worried about him, as there are worse things out there. Thankfully, there aren't any of the operational street lights ahead and the only light comes from the disorienting strobes of red and blue.

He has to risk going out onto the main road, traveling a block down before he can get into the alley that will take him closest to the source of light. He creeps up to the edge of the alley, hunched almost low enough to be on his hands and knees. In the center of the street sits a large SUV with a light bar flashing atop it. The contrast makes it hard to pick out any details, but there doesn't appear to be anyone inside.

He doesn't deflate at the apparent vacancy, forcing himself to consider alternatives, thinking immediately that there is sure to be a radio inside and hopefully a gun of some kind. He can beg forgiveness later. For right now, he needs to worry about his survival. He hefts the hatchet in his right hand, hoping the door is unlocked so that he can avoid breaking the window to gain access.

"All right, fuck it," he mutters out loud. "Here goes nothing."

"I'd stay where you are, if I were you," a calm, commanding voice rises from the shadows, directly behind Hewitt. Startled and acting on instinct, he whips around quickly, swinging the hatchet wildly through the space between himself and the source of the voice while clumsily backing away.

A huge man in a sheriff's uniform steps from the shadows and barely into the pulsing light, effortlessly grabbing the forearm holding the hatchet. Surprised, Hewitt drops the weapon, falling backward on his ass painfully when the man releases his arm. Looming over him in the alley is a man standing easily 6' 5" and weighing a solid 280 pounds. Unexpectedly, the stranger extends his hand.

Hewitt recoils before he recognizes the gesture for the offer of assistance that it is. Cautiously, he takes the hand and is pulled to his feet so rapidly that he almost stumbles and falls all over again.

"You don't want to take the bait," the stranger says. "Trust me."

Hewitt stares at the man, confused and not knowing what to say.

The deputy continues, "There's one of the maniacs in there, crouched down in the passenger side, and he's not alone. He's got friends just out of sight in the shadows across the street." He pauses for a second, appearing to focus on listening for any new sounds. "Guy's name is Jim Stanley, the mechanic from a garage a couple of blocks down. I've known the guy for years. Hell, I even brought my personal truck up here to have him work on it a time or two."

"So, what's going on?" Hewitt asks, finding his voice after another half a minute of silence.

"Near as I can tell," he replies, "Jim and his buddies are waiting to ambush me when I come back to the vehicle. Odds are that encounter won't work out too well for a couple of them, but I'm worried about how it'll work out for me. I think they mean to kill me and I'm dead certain they would've killed you, too."

Sheepishly, Hewitt replies, "I guess I owe you then."

The man takes a moment to look Hewitt up and down. "You're not from around here. Must be why you're acting sane. I'm Deputy Albert Weber, spend part of a rotation here in town at the Emergency Services Building. It's a combination fire department, sheriff's office, and medical clinic near the edge of town."

"My name's Hewitt Chambers and I'm just here visiting a friend."

"That scientist fellow? Price, I believe?"

Hewitt nods while replying, "Yeah. My friends and I came out for vacation, hiking and fishing, that sort of thing."

"Well, I don't know what's going on around here, but you and I are obviously not infected or under the influence, whatever the issue is. There are others who seemed ok too, but guys like Jim out there seem to be hunting them down like animals."

Hewitt's knees almost give out as the unspoken meaning behind the words crash into him, his friends, Mariah. He imagines them being hunted and brought down.

"What do we do?" He finally asks.

"We start by not springing Jim's little trap out there," the deputy replies, gesturing to the street. "I'm thinking you and I make our way up to the old mine and out of this rain for a bit. Gain some high ground and figure out what's next from there."

"I have to get to Gale's house. That's where everyone else was headed," Hewitt protests through clenched teeth.

"I get it that you want to find your friends," Deputy Weber says, his tone managing to convey both sympathy and impatience. "But you ain't running that gauntlet out there and coming through the other side."

Hewitt prepares to argue, but the deputy cuts him off. "I'm not saying we can't go after your friends, but we need to step back and get a handle on whatever this is. You made it this far and maybe they did, too. If they're smart, they'll be doing the same thing we're doing."

It takes him a moment, but Hewitt agrees, nodding his head silently.

"Obviously, we aren't going out this way," the deputy says, gazing out at his vehicle. "How was it back the way you came from?"

Hewitt quickly relates the details of what he'd seen between the rooftop sighting of the lights and his arrival here; not knowing what will be important, he tries to leave out nothing, though he hesitates before admitting to the killing of that man in the alley.

"God damn! That's a hell of a memory you've got there," the deputy replies with a chuckle.

Hewitt grins self-effacingly. "Sort of a thing of mine."

"Good for you," Deputy Weber replies sincerely, bending down and retrieving the hatchet and handing it to Hewitt.

The two of them make their way back down the alley and through town in the opposite direction of where Hewitt knows he should be going.

No amount of caution saves them from being discovered at different points and they do what has to be done, whether facing more of the zombies or small clustered groups of the prowling locals. It certainly doesn't get easier for Hewitt, but he doesn't hesitate like he did the first time. There is no truth for him in the saying that the first time is the hardest as each succeeding murder is no easier.

The men take rest where they can find it, getting to know each other a little better in the process, and they work together as a team, getting through the ordeal of reaching the gravel road leading up to the mine. It's taken them longer than either of them expected but the route was far from straightforward and without obstacles.

"So, what's up there?" Hewitt asks, beaten down by the effort involved in getting just this far.

"Honestly, I have no idea," the deputy replies. "Hopefully, some shelter and a place to catch a second wind so that we can sort shit out. The government was up here years back, sealing up the mine for liability reasons, but I've seen that the opening is still accessible."

"Let's hope you're right."

They begin the ascent, leaving behind the madness of the town and hoping for some peace ahead as they march into the darkness and the unknown.

25

CHAPTER TWENTY-FIVE

WHILE HE CERTAINLY FEELS more confident with the shotgun in his hands, the seven shells won't get him far and the noise is sure to draw all sorts of unwanted attention if he fires them out in the open. He's not willing to trust his luck and count on the locals thinking the blast is just another peal of thunder. That leaves the butcher knife, which won't afford him much protection at all. The thin blade will probably break even if he's careful about how he uses it, and its edge is only good for just the right kind of cutting. It isn't like the movies where some masked serial killer can slaughter a dozen people with the same kitchen blade.

He's better off than he was, he knows, but only marginally so. He would be happy trading both of his current tools for just a single Ka-Bar. At least it would be reliable.

Shit happens, he thinks to himself, *Suck it up, buttercup.*

He's not certain, and the darkness doesn't help, but he believes he's only four or five blocks from Gale's property when he stops to balance himself after hastening away from the house he was certain the enemy would be converging upon. These locals aren't organized or acting like insurgents he's seen overseas, those enemies imitate and emulate the tactics of guerrilla fighters but there is a logic and a structure behind what they do.

This, whatever this is, feels more like a good old-fashioned lynch mob, and that sort of thing correlates with an unsettling cultural heritage that produces a level of discomfort and fear he's never experienced from any of his combat deployments. Gale had brought him out here to cracker country, he and Kateb, and now he's dealing with something that should be buried deep in the shameful depths of American history.

He can't rightly explain the zombies, though. Not by latching onto shit like the KKK or neo-Nazi groups as the culprit, and he's as positive as he can conceivably be that those were zombies. The good ol' George A. Romero variety, just fucking uglier and smelling positively fucking awful. There was none of the cartoonish blue hue or comic book colored blood here, just something horrifying.

He has to resist letting emotion get the better of him, as frustrating and impossible as that seems. As easy as it may be to fall back on this being about his skin color or he and Kateb being gay, that doesn't make any fucking sense with everything else going on. The problem, he finds, is that none of it makes any sense at all. There can't really be zombies.

A trio of locals patrol past his hiding spot and Miles waits for a few beats before slipping from cover into the shadows and following them at what he hopes is a safe distance. Their conversation is lively but he can't make anything out from where he is. He's making better time shadowing these three than he has otherwise and he's starting to feel optimistic about getting to Gale's when a sudden movement ahead, from further down the same lawn he's crossing, causes him to drop to the ground and scuttle for cover.

He's grateful to see that it's the gang ahead of him rather than his presence that set off the zombie. It must have been lurking in the yard, just beyond the bushes that framed the front steps. It latches onto the nearest man of the group and begins tearing into him with gnashing teeth.

The other two don't hesitate as they pry it free from their friend, too late to help him, and begin beating at it with the baseball bats they both carry. The brutality of it forces him to wince as the sounds of skull and bones fracturing are carried to him where he crouches in the dark. The creature is pulverized beneath the force of the blows.

Satisfied with what they've done, they move on, continuing on their way without seeming to care about the man who'd been attacked, leaving him dead, lying halfway on the road without any pretense of remorse or concern. The coldness of the behavior chills Miles more than the cold rain that has soaked into every inch of his clothing. As he sidesteps around the bodies on the ground, he leaves nothing to chance, carefully slipping by with as much space as he can manage between himself and the two unmoving corpses.

He's almost to Gale's when he almost stumbles over a body laying on the ground. In the dark, he hadn't seen it there and as he turns to see what he'd almost tripped over; it lunges for him, useless legs dragging along the ground behind it, using its hands to pull itself along. He steps toward it and slams the knife down into the spine where the skull meets the neck. The blade slides uselessly off of the bone, nearly slicing into his hand in the process.

Still, it does the trick. As ugly and graceless as it might have been, the blade had continued downward, lodging itself into the dirt, slicing through the woman's throat on the way. The zombie on the ground gurgles for a few seconds and then goes still. Miles leaves the knife behind and continues the rest of his way to Gale's house without interruption. There is no sign of activity, but he sincerely hopes that would be true even if everyone had beaten him there.

The front door is locked and he cases the property, making his way around to the rear where nothing but undeveloped wilderness abuts the yard. Cautiously, he approaches the deck overlooking the lawn, and he slides the shotgun up and onto the floor before climbing up the scaffolding, affixing the deck to the edge of the house and hoisting himself silently over the rail. Retrieving the gun, he pads across the deck, peering in through the glass of the French doors.

The patio doors open noiselessly, but he knows anyone listening nearby will hear the change in tone of the rainfall before everything returns to normal. He stands silent and still after closing the door behind him, primed to react if there is any movement. Hushed voices downstairs beckon him and he slips out of his boots, hoping to make less noise.

As he gets closer to the room where the noises are emanating from he recognizes the familiar cadence of Gale's voice and the pitch of Mariah whispering back. Slapping the shotgun over his shoulder as he enters the room, the noise causes both of them to jump.

"I am so glad to see you two," Miles says, with no hesitation. The relief was greater than he'd known it would be. Mariah crosses the space in a flash and hugs him tightly, glancing around him.

"Where's Hewitt?" She asks.

26

CHAPTER TWENTY-SIX

IT'S SLOW GOING, MOVING cautiously while monitoring every shadow the whole way. Abraham begins to worry that he's lost the crowd in the downpour and that they haven't been heading the direction of the city park as he'd suspected they had been.

Hugging the fences and dense shrubbery to keep from standing out in the open during any of the frequent strobes of lighting, as the two of them approach the corner nearest the town's central park. The noise of shouting and screaming becomes audible over the white noise of the storm. Hunkering down, Abraham nudges Ben back against a lilac bush yet to bloom.

As cautiously as they can, father and son creep along the property line toward the corner, the noise from the commotion nearby becoming clearer and muffled largely in waves. A break in the hedge allows them to slip surreptitiously into the corner yard to limit their exposure. From this more secure vantage point, the two of them continue to watch the events unfolding in the park.

There is still no way to make out anything being said, individual words lost in the chaos as the chorus of voices overlap and mingle with the rain. It would have been virtually impossible to mistake the naked hostility for anything else, no matter how difficult it is for Abraham to discern specifics. As the crowd mills about, lit by headlamps, flashlights, and camping lanterns, Abraham can make out what appears to be a scene directly out of an old western or some pre-civil rights documentary.

Nooses are draped from a thick branch on a massive tree, and the ropes are held taut by a person dangling from each snare. From the distance, it's hard to be sure, but neither Abraham nor Ben recognize any of the five people bound and tethered by the neck to the tree. One of the victims appears to be infected by the same illness as that crazy fuck who had killed Kateb, based on the jerking, spasmodic movements and the color of their skin.

There is some relief to be found in the knowledge that the veritable pitchfork-wielding villagers are helping to take out the zombies as well. The enemy of our enemy is not our friend, Abraham knows without any doubt. Without any ceremony or preamble, the benches beneath the hanging victims are yanked away and all five begin a little dance, joining the zombie in an unnatural spasming, a dance that is all too familiar to anyone who's witnessed footage of this method of execution.

Ben stares in fascination and Abraham can't even bring himself to ask his son to look away from the murders taking place. He had already seen worse and there is no reason to think that there isn't worse yet to come. As a father, it is breaking his heart to know that his son will never be innocent again after all of this. It feels like it is taking forever for the executed people to give up the ghost, but finally, the twitches and shakes are done.

The crowd, seemingly satisfied, begins yelling and migrating away from the park grounds, searching for more victims it would seem, without even displaying the decency of cutting down the still hanging people, leaving only the bodies swaying lightly in the wind, suspended as a memento of their presence.

As a pack of nearly a dozen people walks down the sidewalk on the other side of the hedge, Abraham and Ben remain as still as they can manage, holding their breath as a reflex even though there is no reason to think that little bit of noise could give them away. The crowd passes by on the other side of the hedge, only a couple of feet away, and Abraham wishes that he and his son could just merge into the hedge and become invisible. It isn't until the group has moved entirely out of sight and earshot that he even considers moving.

As petrified as they both are, finally they begin to move. The quickest route back to Gale's house will be to cut through the park, but Abraham feels that they are better off going slow and sticking to the lawns and edges of houses wherever possible. He knows that it won't necessarily be any safer, but it isn't worth the risk of being out in the open for too long.

Overall, it's smooth going, aside from a couple of times father and son find themselves hiding while another small mob group shuffles by and one instance when they sit still, terrified because there is a tremendous commotion within the darkness of a house they are skirting by.

It is pure luck that Abraham isn't seen by a crazed woman, bleeding from the corners of her mouth where her lips appear to have been torn wide, staring hungrily through an open front door. She happens to be gazing off to the left when he peeks up from her right before immediately dropping back to the ground and hugging the sodden earth with all of his strength. He crawls slowly back to the edge of the house before he and Ben return to the rear of the yard and move through the neighboring lawn instead.

It's only as they reach and evade staggered groups of people patrolling the streets that they realize they are getting diverted from where they're trying to go. Abraham pulls his son in close and kneels on the ground for a minute, trying to get his bearings and attempting to think through a solution.

Gale's house is not an option, he realizes, considering how drastically they'd gotten turned around. The mine. Gale had told them about the abandoned mine when he was discussing the history of the town. There would be shelter there, somewhere they could dry off and warm up a bit while they sort out the remaining options. It's the next best destination he can think of, the only other destination. They go for it.

———

IT FEELS LIKE THEY'VE spent uncountable hours crossing the town in the opposite direction of their original path. Finally, they are near the main street in what passes for a downtown, near where they started their run from the diner so long before.

Through bursts of light provided by lightning, they can make out the hill, but not the road that leads up to the mine Gale had told them about. They'll find it, though. Hopefully, the others have managed to get through the nightmare gauntlet better than they have and maybe they've all gotten where they all meant to go.

27

Chapter Twenty-Seven

"That's only mildly ominous looking," Hewitt mutters to himself, though the words are overheard by Deputy Albert.

The deputy shivers before replying, "You ain't fucking joking."

The scar on the side of the mountain opens up only about 20 feet from where they stand, a patch of forbidding blackness greater than the surrounding shadows. Neither of them is particularly fond of the thought of crossing the remaining distance to the threshold of that cavernous expanse. After the horrors they'd both witnessed, each of them expects far worse to be awaiting them in the depths of the mine shaft itself.

Hewitt had never been a religious man, and he still finds himself wondering if this isn't some sort of supernatural affliction, demon possession or something like that, the sort of shit he'd seen in movies hundreds of times. The deputy is a religious person and his imagination had taken him that same direction quite some time before. If, from the depths of the mine, Hell was somehow pouring over into the real world, neither man would be particularly surprised.

"So, we should probably just get this over with, for better or worse," Hewitt says. The dryness of his throat and mouth, strange in the abundantly wet surroundings, making the words stick as he attempts to speak.

They move forward almost in unison. The previous hour together had developed a bond of sorts between the two men, something below the level of conscious thought, that place where shared combat instills a sort of brotherhood between men who were previously strangers.As far as either of them knows, they are the only people in town who aren't dead, homicidal maniacs, or zombies.

There's a shared sense of relief as they reach the entrance without hordes of shambling monsters spilling out to meet them and that relief is amplified as they no longer feel the rain tapping out its minor abuse on their heads. Beyond those small blessings, there is no real sense of comfort as they pass beyond the mine's entrance.

Sound works differently just a little way inside. Already tense and nervous, the two of them are tuned in to every little noise, waiting for their eyes to adjust to the pervasive darkness inside the shaft. Neither of them wants the deputy to risk trying his flashlight or cell phone to illuminate the surroundings, both of them irrationally scared of what they might see and knowing that making themselves a target to whoever or whatever might be lurking in the shadows is not a risk worth taking.

It takes Hewitt a minute to realize he's been holding his breath. He exhales as quietly as he can manage. Deputy Albert had been doing the same, and he remembers to exhale when he hears Hewitt doing the same. It is slow, letting their eyes adjust, but finally, they do begin to pick up on some faint details emerging from the blackness around them. The mine appears to be empty as far as they can see, and it certainly should be, based on what the deputy had suggested regarding the place being sealed off to keep local children from being injured if they happened to venture up the hillside.

The deputy taps Hewitt on the shoulder before slipping closer to the wall, gesturing for him to follow. He immediately understands that they are standing out, no matter how dark it is outside if anyone deeper in the mine happened to be looking out. Minimizing their profile is a good move. They both slide to the ground, backs against the rough wall, trying and failing to will themselves to relax for the first time in neither of them can recall how long.

Tense and terrified, they nevertheless begin breathing more deeply after only a few minutes and their heartbeats slow to a more regular and less panicked rate. They shiver from the chill that's seeped its way into them, not just from the rain but from the horrors of the hours leading up to this first moment of peace either of them has experienced. Minds drift, for the first time not focused on surviving what's immediately in front of them, as the two men stop and rest, memories of the experiences eliciting shudders from both of them.

Fight or flight isn't meant to be a sustained state, something both Hewitt and Deputy Albert have come face-to-face with. It exhausts and strains a person in ways no other physical or mental exertion seems to. If Miles were there with them, Hewitt figures, he'd call him a pussy for being so drained.

Miles. He starts to worry about Miles for the first time in an hour or two. Hewitt has never believed in any sort of higher power but he almost starts praying right there, praying that his friends had gotten to Gale's after all and that everyone else was there, together, that they are safe and in a position to relax just like he is right now. Mostly, he knows that he needs Mariah to be safe and that everything hinges on her being ok, at least for his state of mind.

Thinking about Mariah, he wishes he had some way to reach her, to let her know that he's alive and that he's found an ally in the deputy. Mostly, he just wants to hear her voice and to know that she's still out there. He knows that there's no benefit in thinking like that. He has to focus on now on what's in front of him; and what's in front of him is looming darkness and stone and little else. His friends aren't here with him, and he has no way of doing anything about that.

Contrary to what the deputy insisted, there has to be some way out of this godforsaken town. The road can't be all there is. At the very least, they should be able to cut a path through the forest and over the mountains until they reach the road again, somewhere past the flooding river.

"Do you have a family out there?" Hewitt asks, surprising himself. He didn't even know he was going to speak until the words blurted out, surprising him as much as the sound surprises Deputy Weber.

"Nope," he replies. "I'm permanently single. No wife. No kids." He pauses for a moment before continuing, "Parents passed away in an accident years ago, black ice on the highway down near Boise."

"I'm sorry to hear that," Hewitt says.

"No cause for sorry. It's one of those things that happens. It is what it is."

Hewitt nods, knowing how stupid he probably sounded apologizing out of habit. The two men sit together in silence, long enough that they begin to drift in and out of consciousness.

IT COULD HAVE BEEN minutes or it could have been hours. The quality of the light penetrating the mine doesn't appear to have changed when the deputy wakes with a start. Only barely awake himself and momentarily surprised by his companion's startled inhale, Hewitt says, "It's ok. We're still safe here."

Safe. The word almost makes him laugh at having uttered it. There hasn't been a minute of anything like safety in the last 48 hours of his life, perhaps more. The shaft returns to silence as neither of them speaks for a while, slowly bringing themselves back to the real world and wakefulness.

"I'm heading back down there," Deputy Weber says, his voice a clear indication that he wants nothing to do with the thought behind those words.

"You can't be serious?" Hewitt responds.

"Sadly, I really am. I'm not totally fond of the idea of being back down there, but there could be innocent people still in town, and there's no pretending those people aren't in danger."

"I get that, I do, and it's admirable that you want to do something about it. You're just going to get yourself killed out there, though. If there are people alive down there who haven't gone mad, they're probably hiding somewhere too, just like we are."

"It's ok to be scared, Hewitt," the deputy replies. "I'm fucking terrified. But the fact is that I have a job to do."

"I'm not sure your job description includes serving yourself up on a platter to a lynch mob or as dinner for a zombie."

"You've got friends, right? Those friends of yours are still out there somewhere. Don't you want to find them and make sure you're all safe and that you're together?"

Hewitt has no response to that. The words hit him like a hammer between his temples, and he winces in response. He's being a coward, and he knows it. Shame and fear swirl together in his mind. He knows that he should still be out there trying to find everyone. He should be like this cop, trying to save lives and sort out some kind of sense from the nightmare, regardless of the consequence and with no concern for the sacrifice.

He just doesn't have enough left in the tank to go back down there and he knows it. Ultimately, it comes down to the fact that he doesn't want to be left alone here in the dark. Albert may be hardly more than a stranger to him, but at least with the deputy there, he isn't by himself like he had been for too much of the time he spent running through that horror flick brought to life.

"I do," he finally says. "I want that more than I can say. But I can't."

"I'm not asking you to come with me. In fact, I would prefer if you stay put right here. Knowing that you're here, I can feel better about sending any survivors this way if I find anyone who's still sane down there. Maybe I'll even run into those friends of yours."

"You're out of your damn mind, you know?" Hewitt smirks.

"Believe me, I wasn't kidding. I don't want to go back to that place ever again. I've known some of these people for years, maybe not well, but well enough. Witnessing what's been going on there has been devastating."

"I'm sorry for what you've been going through," Hewitt says. "It hasn't really crossed my mind to consider just how different this is, coming at it from the inside. This whole mess has to have been especially trying for you."

"It's certainly nothing I trained for. Hell, I don't think I could have trained for anything like this. But those people down there, they're my responsibility."

Deputy Weber brushes himself off in the darkness, Hewitt barely being able to see anything but the faintest hints of movement.

"Stay safe up here," he finally says, readying himself to venture into the night. "I'll see you again soon, I'm sure."

With that, the deputy steadies himself, nods to Hewitt, knowing that the gesture is likely lost in the shadows, and walks back into the rain and out of the mine. Just like that, Hewitt is alone again. Alone in a dark, abandoned, and empty mine, with nothing but the worst thoughts the recesses of his mind can muster. The situation could be worse, he tries to tell himself, but he's not entirely certain how.

It takes him a while, but he does finally fall asleep again, curled up in the dirt on the floor of the mine, like a baby hoping to be embraced by its mother.

28

— · —

CHAPTER TWENTY-EIGHT

"HEWITT AND I HAD to split up and go our separate ways," Miles says after standing in shameful silence for more than a minute. "There were five of those assholes after us and we had to try to shake them however we could."

"When was the last time you saw him?" Mariah asks.

"It was right after we left the bar," he replies. "We didn't even make it a block before he cut right and I went left."

Mariah steps backward and sits herself down in a chair, slumping, not knowing how to respond. When Miles had walked into the room all full of swagger, she knew Hewitt would be right behind. Hearing that he was still out there somewhere was devastating.

"I'm sorry, Mariah," Miles says. "I really am. I wish he was here with me right now because I hate the thought of him being out there with whatever the fuck is going on."

She says nothing in response and silence fills the room like something permeable, weighted and cloying. The words unsaid are more substantial than anything they could hope to say at this moment. They've all seen horrific things since they left the bar, things that only served to highlight just how awful the situation is. Kateb's death, as horrific and painful as it had been, seems to have been simply the first incident in a night that has become little more than a waking nightmare.

Knowing that Hewitt, Abraham, and Ben are still out there has Miles on edge and he begins pacing the room, desperately trying to think through the whole sequence of events and find some sense in anything that's happened. If he can find some rational or even plausible explanation for everything, maybe he can find some way to get them out of this alive, with the other three in tow. This is who he is, and it's what he does. He doesn't leave anyone behind. Abandoning Kateb is still breaking his heart more and more each time he allows himself to think of his dearest friend laying there on the dingy floor of that bar.

He stands before the window, barely able to make out the distant hints of light where the street lights still glow. There is no movement, and the darkness inside of the home ensures that no one is seeing in. Miles breaks his silence, still staring into the night through curtains of rain.

"Gale, you've been here for a few years now. You know the environment and the people here."

Gale nods, not knowing where this is going.

"We need to get a handle on what we're up against here. We need a map of this fucked up little town and we god damn well need some rough population statistics."

Silence still, as Miles continues staring off into the night.

"I meant fucking now, Gale!" Miles says, turning to look his friend in the eyes. "I'm not sure what you two might have seen on your way here, but this place is well and truly fucked. There's some spooky shit going on out there, and I mean really fucking spooky."

Gale continues staring back, unfocused, no indication he'd even heard what Miles had just said.

Mariah looks up from her seat, pulling out her phone, "I've got a map on here. I had it stored offline since the area wasn't likely to have any kind of stable network access. It's not perfect, but it gives us a bird's-eye view of the streets and businesses. I've got fuckall for statistics, though."

"It's a start," Miles grins.

"I've got maps," Gale finally says. "I have maps, detailed population and demographic statistics, census data, and pretty much everything else you could ask for."

Miles turns to look at Gale again, confused and taken aback by the abrupt response. There's none of the usual self-effacing demeanor present as Gale had spoken, and seeing his friend as seemingly broken and distracted as he's been since Miles made it into the house, he has been feeling like Gale had slipped back into the old mode of being, subdued and timid. Just when he'd been adjusting to the new and improved Gale, seeing the man as he's been the last few minutes felt familiar enough that the return of that self-assured tone is a bit of a surprise.

"Hell, I can provide you with medical histories, NRA memberships, and concealed carry registrations," Gale continues, his voice sounding manic. "I can even pull up education records for every man, woman, and child here."

"What the fuck, Gale?"

Miles isn't the only one stunned by the outburst and slightly frantic tone from their friend. Mariah's mouth hangs open. She has no idea what to say.

Gale inhales deeply before sighing. "Of course, we'd need to get to my lab first, and that means getting through town and making it to the old mine on the other side. It could give us an opportunity to find everyone else though, since I'm worried, they aren't going to be making it back here if they haven't already."

"Wait one second," Mariah interjects. "What are you even talking about? What lab?"

"Did you think I would move somewhere remote like this, somewhere this isolated, without being outfitted to continue my work?" Gale begins, sounding exasperated. "This isn't a vacation home for me, Mariah."

He turns and gestures at the home around them before continuing, "Sure, I still have to travel to CDC headquarters down in Georgia or to various WHO facilities around the country, but I need to be able to work from here as well."

Neither Miles nor Mariah knows what to say. The silence stretches on for an uncomfortable length of time. These new details are difficult to fit into the worldview either of them had up until this point, and something seems out of sync with the fact that they're only now hearing about any of this. Miles stares at Gale, his expression betraying none of the confusion he's experiencing.

"I even occasionally have interns and lab techs staying here in my guest rooms. Why else would I be living in a five-bedroom home like this? Until recently, this place was a sort of hive of activity with other people coming and going, living on my property and working there with me," Gale continues when he realizes no one else is going to speak.

"And this wasn't something you thought to mention to any of us until now?" Mariah asks

"I'm with blondie here," Miles says. "This is exactly the sort of thing that comes up during the usual small talk, catching up with each other portion of the vacation. You know, the sort of thing a regular Joe would include in the conversation."

Gale looks taken aback. "Miles, you of all people understand how my work can be classified in nature. You deal with similar limitations in your own line of work. But the circumstances right now sort of dictate that I can't bother with that sort of concern."

Miles shakes his head, having a difficult time accepting the explanation but not having any real arguments against it. "Well, let's get the fuck out of here and get to this lab of yours. First things first, I want to grab something from the car."

Miles retrieves his keys from the bedroom he and Kateb had shared, changes into dry clothing and a windbreaker that will cut down on the moisture a little bit, and the three of them leave through the front door, watching the shadows for anyone waiting outside.

From the front seat of his car, Miles opens the glove compartment and removes a Colt .45 as well as a second magazine, tucking these into his pocket. He hands the shotgun and the extra five shells to Mariah, after Gale lifts his jacket to display the pistol he's carrying at his waist. He feels much better with a familiar gun in hand and he wants to travel light, so there's no sense in digging through the back just yet. Miles hopes he won't have to worry about the things he has in the back of the SUV, but he has a sinking feeling that he'll be back for the arsenal before this trip is through.

Knowing the town as he does, Gale leads them on a parabolic arc around the edge of the town, mostly through the semi-wooded area and the edges of outlying properties. The people they do happen across are nowhere nearby and of no immediate concern. Miles finds himself wishing he had thought to take a similar route on the way to Gale's house.

They take their time, stepping carefully and watching all around as they go, but the progress is certainly better than any of them made when they were cutting through the town in the aftermath of Kateb's murder.

29

CHAPTER TWENTY-NINE

ABRAHAM AND BEN ARE squeezed into a shadowed alcove in an alleyway when they hear the sound of a firearm being discharged. Three rapid percussions followed by silence. Sounds are tricky at night, in the best of conditions, but it seems to be coming from less than a block away, and they had yet to witness any of the locals using guns during their nocturnal hunting activities.

Abraham feels a surge of hope, wondering if this might be one of his friends. Friend or stranger, whomever it is could be in trouble. He taps his son on the shoulder and gestures the way they've both been peering, the direction he believes the gunshot came from. Ben begins slipping along the wall of the alley, the movements especially silent, the rain masking everything below a whisper.

He pauses at the edge of the alley, allowing his father to slide past him. There's no obvious movement in either direction as he peers through the shadows of the street. The few lights that haven't been damaged and knocked out aren't providing much illumination on this street. He takes a moment to wonder why so many of the lights are gone, probably the locals throwing stones for one reason or another, but he wonders why they would want it any darker than he does.

He's about to dart across the gap to the opposite alley when he sees a shape emerging from the blackness to his left. Quickly, he presses himself against the alley wall and Ben follows his lead. The figure he witnessed was moving silently but not particularly hurried, frequently checking back over his shoulders for some reason.

It's difficult to tell from the distance, but the man appears to be wearing a police uniform of some kind and Abraham stifles the instinctive urge to call out for help from an authority figure. This is no normal night in an average town and there's no reason to think that a cop would provide the usual blanket of security under the present conditions.

Besides, the man is alone; he thinks to himself just before he sees other faint forms showing up suddenly where the cop had previously come from. These people are not trying to exhibit any stealth as they race into the dim lighting of the street.

The cop dodges into the alley where Abraham and Ben were headed only seconds before and Abraham almost missed it, being too distracted by the four new men showing up. It's not difficult to figure out that the solo officer isn't with this group. This is more of the same stalking and hunting behavior he and his son have seen all too much of already.

Being hunted doesn't make the stranger a friend, cop or not, though Abraham isn't prepared to think of any-one in this god awful town as anything but an enemy after everything they've gone through. The cop is good. If Abraham hadn't watched the man fade into the dark-ness of the alley, he wouldn't see the guy at all. He hopes that he and Ben are as well shrouded in their position, especially as the angry group of locals gets closer.

These new men sound angry. Everyone they've heard sounds like they're enraged. The snippets of voices reaching Abraham's hiding place are fueled by the same manic hostility they've been hearing all night. The cop may be another bad guy, for sure, but these men were monsters.

They pause briefly, abreast the alley, peering left and right. Abraham feels Ben tense up and shiver beside him and he knows its not from the chill in the air that's penetrated them both to the core. The way those crazed assholes are gazing into the deeper darkness of the alley, Abraham is sure they'll be running for their lives all over again any second. He's tensed in preparation for what he knows is a race he lacks the energy to run.

He's almost ready to bolt, refusing to wait until they come at him when they finally begin moving down the street again. He releases the breath that had been hurting his lungs. His momentary relaxation is devastated as he jumps at the sound of nearby gunfire. It's been no more than a couple of seconds and he didn't see the cop lean from his hiding place in the alley after the party had passed.

The man is insane, but two of the four roving locals are on the ground. One is pretty clearly down and not getting back up, but the other is trying to rise and follow his two uninjured friends as they speed toward where the cop is now standing. Another steady shot and the closest of the two predators is down.

Fully a quarter of the man's face seems to have disappeared in a flash. The man still approaching the cop doesn't seem to care, and he leaps the remaining distance to the officer, swinging wildly with what appears to be a large kitchen knife. Only a fraction of a second to think about doing something.

If Abraham had more time to think things over, he might have reacted differently, but his better nature wins out and he runs from the alley, first toward the injured man finally regaining his feet and lurching rapidly toward the conflict in the middle of the street. His foot connects solidly with the side of the slower man's knee, and he falls back to the wet pavement with a loud huff. The way the knee looks now, the local won't be standing or walking again, perhaps ever.

Abraham turns to face the struggle still taking place, the cop desperately trying to hold off the madman astride him, but he can't compete with the lunatic's strength and frenzy. It's hard to tell in the middle of the commotion, but the officer appears to already be injured. The darkness and all the motion makes it a challenge to discern blood from water at the distance.

He's never been a weak man, and he still works hands-on at many of his job sites, but he feels like he's wrestling with a bear like some Russian circus performer as he grabs the man from behind and struggles to pull him from the cop on the ground. He's praying the whole time that the cop keeps his hand locked around the wrist of the hand holding the knife, keeping the blade in sight and away from him.

The officer uses the new shift in momentum and pushes with the last bit of strength in reserve to drive the knife into the chest of his assailant, holding it there until the man's weight is finally removed thanks to Abraham's efforts in pulling the dying man back.

It takes the deputy a minute to catch his breath before he looks quizzically at the man who just rescued him and the boy now standing beside him and slightly behind. "You must be Hewitt's friends. A couple of them at least," he says in a hoarse whisper. "I don't recognize you and I'm at least mostly familiar with the locals hereabouts."

Abraham doesn't miss a beat, his excitement bursting forth in his words, "You've seen Hewitt! Where is he?"

Deputy Weber laughs. "I left him up in the mine shaft, back that way," he gestures behind him, the direction he'd come from only a short while before. "Straight shot from here to a gravel road. If you keep going back that direction, it's impossible to miss."

He winces as he tries to stand, attempts to push through the pain, and falls back to the ground. Feeling around where his pain is located, his hand comes away wet, which doesn't surprise him, but it also comes away dark with blood, which isn't much of a surprise anymore either.

"Fucking asshole actually did some damage," he says as he looks down from where he sits at the man sprawled on the ground near his feet. "God damn it, Walter," he continues, more amused and fascinated than anything else.

Abraham and Ben lean down to help him up to a more upright position before dragging him off to the edge of the brick building to the same side of the alley where the deputy had been hiding only a couple of minutes ago. In the faint light available to them, it's still difficult to miss the way the blood seems to be surging, flowing with the rhythm of the deputy's weakening pulse. Abraham's never been great with biology or anatomy, but he's seen plenty of injuries on the job and he recognizes a severed artery when he sees it.

Father and son sit down beside Deputy Weber and they discuss the events of the last couple of days. With the deputy's insight, it looks like things have been getting weird around town since before Kateb's murder the evening before. Townspeople appeared to be going crazy in the days leading up to the insanity now manifested in town. Finally, after longer than Abraham believed he would last, the deputy slumps where he's sitting in mid-sentence.

He and Ben peek out at the street to make sure they're unobserved. The directions to the gravel road leading to the mine are as easy to follow as Deputy Weber led them to believe. The distance isn't great, but having to evade the occasional prowling locals slows them down.

The road leading its winding way up the hill is ill-maintained and the uneven surface is treacherous in the dark. Twists and switchbacks as the elevation increases lead to a much greater delay than either of them anticipated. When the pitch black of the entrance appears, Abraham catches himself grabbing Ben by reflex and pulling him closer, suddenly certain that this is some kind of trap.

If Hewitt is in there, he is surely dead, and his son will be dead as well if they go in there, too. Deputy Weber had seemed earnest and sincere, even kind, but everything lately had been so topsy-turvy. If it was a trap, Abraham figures after some quiet deliberation, there's no sense in not walking right into it.

The two of them slowly pass through the portal and feel immediate relief that there's no more rain falling on them. It certainly isn't warm inside, but it's comparatively dry, at least in relation to the outside. Abraham stops, uncertain, trying to penetrate the darkness with his gaze.

"Hewitt?" he whispers, his voice carrying much better than he meant for it to. No echo. Only silence. A full minute passes and there's a rustle somewhere up ahead. The distinctive scuff of something sliding over dirt and gravel. Sure that there's another one of the zombies on the approach, perhaps dozens or even hundreds of them, Abraham prepares to run back the way they came.

"Abraham, is that you?" Hewitt inquires, as he tentatively walks toward the entrance.

"You're damn right it is!" Abraham stumbles forward in the shaft, dragging Ben along in his wake, slowly making sense of the silhouette of his friend emerging from the surrounding shadows.

"Thank fucking Christ!" Hewitt exclaims as he rushes forward the remaining distance to embrace his friend.

Being sheltered from the rain, there is no mistaking that there are tears on Hewitt's cheeks, but it's too dark and he is far too relieved and grateful not to be alone that he doesn't care to try to hide his emotional response.

30

CHAPTER THIRTY

The relief in the cavern is palpable as the friends compare their experiences since separating at the bar the evening before. Though it hasn't been 24 hours since the events at the diner had transformed the vacation into a nightmare, it feels like they've lived through so much.

Hewitt responds as if he's taken a blow when Abraham tells him what happened with Deputy Weber and how he and Ben had remained tucked away in hiding, too uncertain of the situation to act until it had been too late. He and the deputy had bonded more than he'd realized until that moment, during the hours they'd spent together, relying on one another to survive. Hewitt winces as he hears the detailed admission from his friend that the man's death had been avoidable, but he knows that Abraham made the right, probably the only, choice at the time. It was the only thing that made any sense for them to do. He had his son to worry about, and with the lunacy unleashed within the town, the risk was too great.

Still, it pains him to know the man is gone. Deputy Albert Weber had struck Hewitt as being a good man, someone he could respect and maybe even admire, and his death just meant that there was one less person to fight the rising tide of insanity threatening to wash them all away with the floodwaters.

He finds himself shifting focus to the fact that Abraham and Ben are the only friends he's seen since Kateb's murder led them to striking out on their own. With the deputy dead, he worries that no one will find them here in the mine, assuming anyone else is alive and in any condition to search for them. Relief fades into defeat just like that, as he allows himself to consider the very real possibility that the three of them might be the only ones left alive.

He knows these thoughts, the flickering voices in the back of his head whispering terrifying possibilities. It's a concerted effort of willpower for him to even begin shifting the focus away from those awful thoughts. It's difficult for him to imagine Miles falling to the violence out there while he somehow managed to make it through the night. Mariah was more suited to survival as well, he reminds himself. She's certainly a more effective hunter than he is.

Gale may be soft, but he's sly, and he knows the area, which has to give him some advantage. He was with Mariah the last time they'd seen each other as well, and she would keep him safe. They would keep each other safe. The only way he won't go mad with desperation and grief is to keep reminding himself that his friends out there are better equipped for the situation than he is. The whole thing had snuck up on them. It was a surprise for Kateb, for all of them, when that first incident had happened, but it wasn't a surprise to any of them anymore.

In the darkness of the tunnel, happy to be with his friend and Ben, he can't seem to stop himself from feeling the fear and uncertainty eating away at him and all he can do is persistently fight the emotional turmoil that threatens to shake him to pieces. Abraham, to his credit and quite unlike Hewitt, is focused on how relieved he is that the three of them are together. Things may continue to get worse, and it looked like they probably would, but at least they wouldn't be alone for whatever was still coming.

His faith in their friends out there is as unshakeable as it ever was and it's natural for him to simply assume that everyone else is back at Gale's house, settled in and formulating a plan to get them all out of this awful place. For Abraham, there are none of the dark thoughts that haunt his friend. Gale knows the area and Miles knows combat scenarios, so it stands to reason that their stay in the mine will be a brief one.

He had always been an optimist and the present circumstances, as dire as they might be, aren't sufficient to erode that positivity in his nature. Having a child had only seemed to shore up the man's inherent optimism. It was the perspective he wanted to instill within his children.

The two friends, as close as they'd always been, couldn't have been more diametrically opposed as far as their mental states were concerned. They had always been that way, and they complemented one another well in most situations.

In the present circumstances, Abraham's proactive impulse reinforces Hewitt's discomfort with remaining so close to the entrance as the three of them decide to risk exploring deeper into the mine just to be on the safe side. In case some of the locals make their way up the hill, anyone with a flashlight would see them where they presently are and that is simply not good.

As it turns out, Abraham is the only one with any charge left on his cell phone. Hewitt's had been damaged during his escape through the town, and Ben's had been dead before they'd even left the bar. Not that the devices would've been good for much, with no signal available. But they could at least provide some much-needed illumination.

The flashlight mode isn't great, but it's more light than any of them had experienced for several hours. The tunnel looks exactly as they expected; compacted dirt, well-worn on the floor, with stones and large slivers of wood peppering the ground here and there. Predictable passages or not, they take it slowly, looking around with a sort of paranoid expectation that something awful awaits them in each shadowy nook.

Hewitt is the first to notice that something seems off. It seems to him as if the murmur of the rainfall from outside has somehow changed in tone, like a gentle hum. He would almost swear he can feel it, in the ground or the air around them. The walls and floor seem to be cleaner, more uniform as they venture further into the mountain.

He doesn't know much about caves or mining, but he assumes it has something to do with them being in a more stable environment as they move further away from the outside world. *Maybe,* he thinks, he recalls something, *there is some equilibrium or homeostasis in caverns.* It could be something along those lines, but he doesn't know where he remembers it from or whether he can trust his recollection as being entirely accurate.

Hewitt may have been the first of the three to recognize that something is different, that something seems wrong, but it's Ben who first says something about it.

"Do you hear that whine?" the boy asks, looking around them for the source of a sound only he hears.

Neither his father nor Hewitt hear the noise, their ears not being as sensitive to the specific pitch of it, but both of them can feel that something is different in the air, and the smell of it isn't right either. It should be smelling more earthy and stale, Hewitt suspects. Abraham is thinking similar thoughts, remembering family visits to caverns when he was growing up.

"I don't hear anything, kid, but something sure smells wrong about this place."

"Should we turn around?" Ben asks, feeling uncertain as he looks back at Hewitt in response.

He thinks for a few seconds before replying, "We probably should, but that's not what we're going to do, are we, gentlemen? I may regret saying it, maybe soon, but I doubt whatever's ahead of us can be worse than what we left behind."

"God damn it, Hewitt," Abraham mutters, stifling a reflexive laugh. "Why do you always say shit like that?"

"I don't know, man. It's a nervous habit."

"You have always pulled that kind of shit since we were kids," Abraham says, still trying not to laugh at the absurdity of it all. "You are always getting us in trouble, jinxing us with that bullshit, testing fate."

"Whistling past the graveyard, maybe?"

"That is not better," Abraham whispers.

They continue in silence, slowly making their way down the tunnel. Uncertain of what might await them just beyond the meager cone of light shed by the cell phone, they take their time. The light doesn't reveal much, but there doesn't appear to be much to see. Abraham begins to hear a slight hum. He's not sure if he even really hears it, so faint is the sound. It's almost more than he feels it.

Moments later, Hewitt reaches out to his shoulder to stop him. "Do you hear that?"

Abraham nods and so does Ben.

Their already creeping pace slows even further as they approach what appears to be a bend in the shaft ahead of them. The noise becomes gradually louder and more discernibly mechanical as they approach the source. Hewitt has goosebumps accompanying the chills he feels as they get closer to the corner in the shaft. The tunnel appears to take on a faint red glow, his mind playing tricks on him as his heart rate rises with each step. The others see the same thing, but they each assume it's just them as well.

There is no response but confusion. As they reach the corner and their adventure into the unknown becomes something far more perplexing.

Filling the tunnel ahead of them, only feet away, is a concrete platform leading up to a wall of the same material spanning the height and width of the shaft. They've all seen enough movies and television shows that they recognize a hermetically sealed door with a mesh grate above it where a fan is circulating out of sight, pulling the air from the mine into whatever space might be beyond the door. Now that they know to look for it, they can just barely perceive the suction as the air is pulled past them in the space surrounding where they stand.

To the right of the door is a key card reader with a dot of red light illuminating the immediate area. Whatever this place is, it has power.

"Well, this is unexpected," Hewitt says, unable to wrap his head around what he's seeing after staring for a minute or more.

"Unexpected, but not entirely all that surprising, you know, considering everything else," Abraham replies.

Both men chuckle nervously in response, Ben watching them as if they've lost their minds, and there they stand at a dead-end presented by a massive industrial door that opens on what, they can't even imagine.

ABRAHAM'S PHONE FINALLY DIES, leaving the three of them with only the ghostly red light to illuminate the already surreal and spooky surroundings.

To Hewitt, watching his friend and his son sleep, it looks like he is seeing the world through a film of blood, or like everything surrounding him has been covered in it. Considering events, he wonders which analogy would be the more à propos.

Seconds, minutes, maybe hours later, he can't begin to measure the passage of time. Hewitt feels his exhaustion dragging his eyelids together, and he figures there's no harm in letting go. He wouldn't be any better off awake than asleep, he figures, when whatever comes next finally leaps out at them to drag them kicking and screaming into the grave. At least asleep, he might not see it coming or feel it when it hits.

31

CHAPTER THIRTY-ONE

"SOMETHING IS VERY WRONG here," Miles mutters as they step further into the cavernous darkness, away from the rain and the wind outside.

"Thanks for clarifying the situation for us so eloquently, Mr. Thousand-yard stare. Care to provide any additional astonishing insights?" Mariah replies with a smirk. She's desperately hoping the lighthearted ribbing might be sufficient to keep Miles from dwelling too much on what had happened at the diner. She's been trying to avoid thinking about it, herself.

Miles looks around at the dirt and stone surrounding them, taking in the details, skeptical for the first time that Gale has led them astray for some unknown reason. It could be that their friend is just as mad as the rest of the people in this horrible town, and this is a ruse inspired by that madness. It's difficult to imagine anything like that being true, but the whole damn night has been difficult for him to wrap his head around and he was nowhere near being able to come to terms with or make sense of this.

Mariah is similarly confused by what she's seeing, just another mine shaft carved into the wall of the mountain, no different from any other she's seen in photographs or on screen. This certainly doesn't appear to be a lab of any kind she's ever seen.

"Gale, my friend," Miles begins, glancing to the side where their friend is standing, "I'm not seeing any fucking laboratory here."

Gale smiles knowingly and begins walking ahead of them confidently, not even acknowledging the surroundings. "It would hardly be a secret facility if anyone who glances in from the outside could see that it's here."

With no choice but to follow his lead, Miles and Mariah begin to trail after their friend, neither of them sure of his intentions or his state of mind. Neither of them is even particularly sure of their own states of mind, having had no chance to sit back and process everything that's happened, from Kateb's murder to this walk down an empty mineshaft toward the unknown.

Mariah speaks more to break the uncomfortable silence than anything else. "What sort of lab are we talking about here, Gale?"

"Well, you know the line of work I'm in," Gale begins and then pauses, neither of his friends even knowing whether he'll be saying anything further or if that was the end of the statement as far as Gale was concerned. He had always been a bit odd and prone to trailing off as other things came to mind. Neither of them would have been surprised if that was the case this time.

Finally, after a matter of a few seconds, he does continue, "Virology mostly. There are surprisingly few facilities out there where biosafety level four research can be performed. There are a lot of conditions that absolutely must be met before it's even remotely safe to work with the sort of things requiring BSL-4 security."

Mariah looks around. "And you're saying that this is one of those places?"

"Absolutely," Gale replies. "The mine goes deep, very deep, into the mountain, which makes securing the location surprisingly simple. We're in a tectonically stable region with only a small population and limited visibility to potential terrorists."

Miles had some experience with nuclear, biological, and chemical training through his time in the military, and he understands a little bit of what Gale is explaining as he continues telling them about how and why the CDC had decided on this location. Mariah has some passing familiarity with these things as well, though mostly from fiction and research for the courses she's taught.

They travel deeper into the mine shaft, going further than they expected before they see what appears to be a bend in the tunnel. Conversations taper off naturally, as all three of them develop varying degrees of apprehension regarding what could await them just around the bend. Blind corners have not been friendly to them lately. In silence, the final few meters, they continue forward, Miles checking the chamber of his pistol in preparation for what could be ahead of them.

ABRAHAM, BEN, AND HEWITT wake almost simultaneously to the sound of hushed and indistinct voices. Too freshly awakened, they all start, producing numerous scraping and scrambling noises of their own, causing Hewitt to wince and hold his breath reflexively. The approaching voices and now audible footsteps continue heedless, either not hearing or not caring about the noise the three of them produced in their surprise.

Abraham and Hewitt slowly rise to their feet, nudging Ben behind them. They steel themselves for the conflict they know is coming. The odds are not in their favor, both of them are well aware of this, but if any of these crazy locals want to get their hands on Abraham's son, they are going to have to fight through the two of them to get there.

Their eyes have adjusted to the red glow from the access panel, and they begin to see evidence of flashlights or some other similar light sources bouncing around on the wall ahead of them, where the tunnel bends to the left and continues mostly straight to the exit.

The wobbling, inconsistent glow gets brighter on the tunnel wall. The voices and shuffling sounds of movement grow louder, but the way the noises echo in the mine makes it impossible to decipher anything being said or even how many voices are contributing to the sound.

It could just be wishful thinking on his part, but Hewitt believes it's only a few people, only five or six at most, and at least they're not the zombies. None of the few he'd seen while escaping through the town appeared capable of communicating, or maybe they just hadn't wanted to talk to him. He was assuming the former to be the case.

The downside, he figures, is that they'll be armed. For the fifth or sixth time since Kateb's death, he finds himself mentally comparing the people of the town to the angry villagers from the old Frankenstein movie. He imagines a group of the townsfolk coming around the bend with lanterns and pitchforks, and he realizes he won't even be the least bit surprised if that is precisely what he is about to see.

Tensed to react, both men remain steady and unflinching as the intruders round the corner and the glare of flashlights blind them. Of all the eventualities Hewitt and Abraham had prepared themselves for, what neither of them anticipated was the simultaneous cacophony of both Mariah and Miles calling out their names in combined pleasure and disbelief.

The disbelief and uncertainty in those two voices doesn't match what Abraham, Ben, and Hewitt find themselves feeling in response. As wound up and prepared for violence as both men had been, it's a challenge to shift gears with the sudden shock. Finally, they do deflate and the tension they'd both been holding in is released in shivers.

"It's great to see you guys," Hewitt says, with a grin spreading across his face. "Or maybe it would be, but we can't see shit with those lights in our eyes."

32

— · —

Chapter Thirty-Two

Relieved embraces are exchanged as they all let go of the fear and strain they'd been carrying with them, afraid they would never see each other again.

"What in the hell are you guys doing here?" Abraham asks, disrupting the brief pleasantries. He's been wondering that very thing since the initial shock of seeing them there had worn off. There seems to be no logical reason for them to all be in the mine unless something had gone horribly wrong or they had been herded here, much like he worried he and Ben had been.

Hewitt raises his left eyebrow but almost immediately begins following a parallel thought process to what Abraham had already been thinking. The logistics involved in how and why their friends had also found themselves driven to the mine could have some dramatic implications, depending on what those reasons were. The three new arrivals and Ben all react with differing degrees of confusion to the edge in Abraham's voice, only Hewitt having stumbled upon the same conclusion in his quick analysis.

Miles reaches over and gently shoves Gale forward. "Apparently, our buddy Gale has managed to bring his work home with him in a big way."

The smile on Miles' face is sincere enough, but there's a visible tightness in the expression, visible even in the poor lighting conditions, that betrays something else beneath the surface. Hewitt figures they'll get to that in due time. For the moment, there are too many other questions flooding through his mind.

"So," he begins, gesturing toward the wall obstructing the tunnel, "is this your doing then?"

"Well, it's not entirely my doing, but it is my lab behind that door," Gale replies with a nervous smile.

"Let's get the fuck in there then, before anyone else joins our little powwow here," Hewitt says with a touch of excitement.

Gale doesn't miss a beat as he walks forward, brandishing a rectangular keycard attached to a chain hanging around his neck that he's pulled from his shirt. He waves the card before the scanner and the light turns from red to green. There is no audible beep like the group was expecting, and there is no thunking click signifying a lock being disengaged. Everything is silent beyond their nervous breathing and shuffling feet. Movies and television had ruined them all in some sense, establishing false expectations regarding high-tech security doors.

Gale takes the handle and pulls the door outward without fanfare and they all feel a burst of air flowing past them and into the brilliant white space that appears before them as lights turn on automatically. Six pairs of eyes squint in response to the sudden increase in illumination. Gale doesn't wait for anything and he crosses the threshold like he had hundreds of times before, falling back on familiarity and routine for comfort under the awful conditions they find themselves here.

The others don't immediately follow, requiring more time to process the new space ahead of them and react accordingly. Ben is the first to follow after Gale, rushing into the new space with no small amount of enthusiasm. Abraham follows, spurred into action by his son. Miles goes next and Mariah after that, first glancing back at Hewitt to see what he's doing. He stands there, watching his friends pass beyond the entrance into something alien and unfamiliar.

He should be used to those things by now, having been thrust into a series of events that have boggled his mind to no end. There is no safety to be found here, he finds himself certain of that fact, but at least they'll be together. Finally, Hewitt follows, pulling the steel and concrete door closed behind him, absently marveling at how smoothly it sways on the hinges. With a faint hiss of air pressure equalizing, the world outside is shut away.

Hewitt feels no relief, unable to shake the sense of dread that the worst is still to come.

33

⸻ ◆ ⸻

Chapter Thirty-Three

Mathematics and the sciences had always been Gale's greatest focus throughout school. In everything else, he frequently required some assistance, in the form of tutoring from his friends or supplemental learning materials, but in math and science, he was golden.

Tristan and Hewitt were his usual go-to's for the tutoring or anything along those lines because they could not only help him to shore up the areas where he was lacking, but they could speak a language he had no trouble following. It helped that they never seemed to require any assistance at all, everything coming easily to those two.

If he'd been a different sort of person, he might have envied the two of them their ability to integrate things the way they did; he just didn't have the capacity to be jealous, apparently. Instead, he marveled at their capacities to comprehend things that managed to elude him and to convey those concepts and facts in a form that he could somehow understand.

Gale remained at home with his parents after high school, commuting close to an hour, either way, to attend university nearby. His parents had been an older couple when they had him and neither of them was in great health by the time he was in his third year of college.

During the day, while he was in class, a nurse was in the home with his mother and father and he spent his evenings balancing homework and caring for his parents. While his affect may have appeared distant and often detached, he cared deeply for his family and it showed in the level of care he was sure to provide for them.

When they passed away, it was within weeks of one another, his mother only a week after Halloween and his father just before mid-terms of his senior year of college. As an only child, he was left to plan the funeral arrangements on his own. Compartmentalization was the only thing that made it possible for Gale to manage all of these duties while not missing more than the couple of days of school that were absolutely unavoidable. He'd displayed a knack for being able to emotionally disconnect from everything in his life a long time before, bordering on repression at times; but he always seemed to function well enough that no one ever worried too much about his state of mind.

Mariah, Hewitt, and Tristan all managed to attend both funerals. The other three friends were unable to get leave or afford travel arrangements for their friend's sake. In the cases of Abraham, Miles, and Kateb, cards were sent and phone calls were made. Gale appreciated the support and the attempts to provide comfort, even though he felt like he was coping with the situation well. He knew it would have been a challenge for everyone to make it.

Hewitt and Tristan made a habit of checking in on him regularly through the rest of winter and the following spring, opting to occasionally work on their homework and studies at Gale's house, around the same kitchen table where they'd often done the same during their youth. Silent and separate from one another, they did their best to be there for their friend without needing to say a word a lot of the time.

The house was on the market and readied for sale a week after Gale's graduation. Between life insurance and the sale of the house, he was able to move on for further education, set in his objective to never stop learning. As it turned out, he didn't need the money as much as he'd imagined. He was awarded a partial scholarship to the biology graduate program at MIT and a research assistant position to supplement the remaining costs.

The work kept him busy and his course load led him to a Ph.D. program in the brain and cognitive sciences where he excelled. With the extra course studies he'd added to his required curriculum, paying out-of-pocket for additional classes just to improve his versatility, Gale was only twenty-nine years old when he began working full time with the Centers for Disease Control.

During graduate school, he had already started working on projects funded through the CDC and the World Health Organization, but his association was made official upon graduation. He moved down to Atlanta, GA that summer and, in the fall, began taking additional classes in molecular and cell biology to increase his overall value in the position he held.

It was no surprise to any of his friends that Gale was well-respected and successful within his field and no one who knew him was shocked that he was making a name for himself within the circles of the CDC and WHO. Over the years in college, he had managed to pick up a thing or two from his more socially oriented and adroit friends, and he played politics well within those organizations.

Tristan's suicide hit him hard. After returning from the funeral, his work became more focused and driven, impressing everyone above him as he threw himself more completely into his work to escape from the nearly overwhelming sense of loss he felt at losing someone closer to him than his parents had been. More compartmentalization, more suppression, and repression.

Healthy or not, Gale did what he always did when he needed to cope. He immersed himself further in work and study, displaying no outward signs of the strain he was under. He was coping in the only way he knew how, and it worked for him better than it probably would for most.

His friends, were they were around, might have recognized some telltale signs of Gale shutting down, some minuscule cracks showing in the veneer of the professional detachment he wore like a second skin, but they rarely heard from him during the intervening years until they all received the special invitations.

34

— · —

CHAPTER THIRTY-FOUR

THE GROUP LOOKS AROUND in stunned silence as they pass through the second pressurized door, all except Gale, who walks through the entrance space to flip the rest of the interior lights beyond the airlock from emergency lighting to the overhead fluorescents. With that transition, banks of computer monitors and other equipment begin to power on as well, the buzzing and humming of hard drives and electricity completing circuits fill the air. Even Gale needs a few seconds for his eyes to adjust to the new lighting.

From the room they stand in, Hewitt feels like they are only seeing the tip of the iceberg. There's something about the way the noises reverberate within the space that makes him feel like they are in only a small component of a much larger facility. As he squints against the glaring lights, he takes in what he can with his other senses. There is a definite thrumming vibration all around, carried from unseen machinery through the walls and floor and directly to his nerves. It feels like something alive, albeit in hibernation.

It smells like a hospital, but not quite. There is that same sterile, antiseptic quality in the odors, but not quite the smell of life and death that is typical of those places. This is no hospital, he reminds himself. There is none of the pretense of being warm and welcoming that one normally finds in a hospital, as often as those buildings fail in that regard.

Gale breaks the overall silence by leafing through papers in a steel drawer before pulling out a map that he spreads out on top of the stainless steel table that seems more appropriate for a veterinary clinic than the office-like environment they're in presently.

"I told you I had a map of town up here," he says proudly as he gestures to Miles.

Miles scoffs before shaking his head. "Asshole, I think we have bigger questions here than to be concerned about whether you actually had a map up here."

Mariah chuckles momentarily before catching herself.

"Miles is right," Hewitt pipes up. "What is this place?"

"This is where I worked until very recently," Gale replies. "You don't think I commuted to Atlanta from Idaho for work all the time, do you?"

"This is fucking crazy, though," Hewitt says, gesturing all around at the virtually cavernous room they're standing in. "How could something like this be built without everyone knowing about it?"

"People in town were well aware of the construction taking place up here, just not what was involved or the ultimate purpose of it. As far as any of the locals knew, the Bureau of Land Management was here to seal the mine for safety reasons. The land was already owned by the US government. I simply had a proposal on the table that they considered viable."

Gale continues, telling his friends about how the CDC had been searching for a new location to establish another BSL-4 facility in a geologically stable location and the existing mine in this region provided an excellent scaffold from which it could be assembled. The National Science Foundation, he explained, had already provided proof of concept for just this sort of thing by converting a former gold mine in South Dakota into a series of different labs at various levels underground. It was a major cost-saving measure for the CDC to simply take advantage of the existing structure of the mine.

"No one," he assures them, "outside of Washington DC and the CDC even knows that this place exists, except for you now."

Gale goes on, explaining that the place is powered by a geothermal plant over the rise of a nearby mountain that is largely automated and designed to run with minimal human involvement. The same plant supplies power to the emergency systems down in the town and in some other neighboring areas, a concession made to the locals when the construction was going on up the hill in the former mine. All they knew was that the BLM was offering some new enhancements to the power grid due to the amount of energy they were drawing during the construction process.

"The reality was," he continues, "that we needed to justify the presence of so much Department of Energy staff as well as representatives of the NSF being present for something as seemingly straightforward as filling an empty mine with concrete."

It comes as a surprise to all of them that Gale has been splitting his time between Idaho, Atlanta, and D.C. For more than seven years, he was placed in charge of this facility and he oversaw aspects of the construction and development. Until just then, none of his friends had grasped just how much pull Gale had within the CDC, and they were all taken aback that he could be involved with something this massive and clandestine.

"You played this one close to the chest, didn't you?" Miles asks, patting his friend on the back as he makes his way from the table where the map is spread out to a computer monitor displaying a flickering image with a slightly green tint to it.

Hewitt is feeling a sinking sensation in the pit of his stomach and he can't quite place the reason why. Something is wrong, he thinks to himself, or maybe he's finally dealing with the side-effects of everything he's experienced since Kateb had been killed. Of course, something is wrong, he tells himself. Everything has been wrong for a little while now. He chuckles to himself, amused by the absurdity of only suddenly realizing that nothing was right about the last twenty-four hours or longer.

"Holy shit!" Miles says, pointing at the monitor that had captured his attention. "Are these fucking security cameras, Gale?"

"Of course they are," his friend replies. "We have cameras all through the lab, hidden in the mine shaft through the door back there, and all around near the entrance to the mine itself. You have no idea what sort of security is required for this sort of facility to get off the ground."

Miles chuckles absently and returns his attention to the monitor, watching as the image transitions from the feed of one camera to another.

Gale, sidetracked by Miles' interruption, begins telling them about the security precautions that went into place when this lab was being constructed. In the back of his mind, Hewitt begins to wonder why, if there's so much stringent security required, there are no other staff members around. He worries that he might already know the answer and that the staff usually in place here is down there in town, running wild with the locals and murdering people.

He's remained calm and even-tempered throughout most of what's transpired, but Hewitt's coping mechanisms are frequently unhealthy and he's starting to find perverse amusement with the scale of just how badly everything has gone.

"Zombies, check. Mobs of angry villagers, check. No cell phone service, check. No rescue en route from emergency services or the National Guard. Big fucking check." Hewitt mumbles to himself as he wanders in circles around the large open space of the lab beyond the second set of doors leading in from the mine itself.

Everyone is coming to terms with the changing situation in their own ways now that they've got a chance to decompress and catch their breath. Hewitt isn't even taking in the surroundings at this point, muttering and talking to himself while he works through the trauma and circumstances that led them to where they are. Gale stops talking mid-sentence as Hewitt's rambling interrupts his discussion of the security protocols.

Mariah watches him, concerned about his state of mind but knowing that this is just the way he does things.

"Of course, it's got to be raining. It's always raining when the world comes to an end. This is just altogether too fucking typical," Hewitt continues as he paces back and forth, desperately trying to analyze what has happened, striving to discern some sort of solution that is eluding him but that he feels is looming right there at the edge of his perception.

Miles glances up from a computer monitor where he's been compulsively watching the changing perspectives of the cameras outside that they'd seen no evidence of when they'd made their way into the mine even though they could see the path they'd taken not more than half an hour before. Even knowing that some of the town is on a backup power supply and that the lab itself is independently powered he is still surprised that this place is entirely untouched by the power outage throughout the town itself, "Are you trying to make a joke right now, Hewitt? We watched Kateb getting torn into pieces by what we all seem to swear was a goddamn zombie no more than twelve hours ago, and that's not even the only one I've seen since then, and you consider this an opportunity to try to be cute or funny?"

Gale shakes his head, dispelling whatever inner musings he was entertaining until that moment. "Could you please just calm down, both of you? We have more important things to worry about, I do believe."

"Don't you fucking tell me to calm down! You saw the same damn things that I did, the same damn things all of us saw," Miles growls without looking away from the screen displaying the drowning world outside.

Hewitt can't shake the feeling, and it's been getting distressing the whole time Gale has been talking, that things are still heading downhill and that everything will get worse before it gets better, assuming it ever does get better. The clean, sterile laboratory environment feels unreal after spending so much time in the rain and the filth of the town itself. It doesn't make sense, something like this located in the veritable middle of nowhere.

Miles is certain, without any niggling doubts, that there is a clear correlation between the events of the last couple of days and what he's seeing here in this facility. The others all share those thoughts, he's sure, at various places along the same mental steps he's making. Miles is a few steps ahead of his friends though, shock and combat trauma being things he's been acquainted with for his whole adult life because he does not doubt that Gale knows more about this than he's letting on. He continues watching the screen, occasionally glancing back at his friend while he rambles on about how great this facility happens to be.

Hewitt is putting two and two together as well, not far behind Miles, in his own disorganized fashion, finding it altogether too coincidental that their biologist friend would just happen to be living somewhere so isolated, working in some secret lab sitting nestled in the corpse of a decommissioned mine. He's no scientist himself, but he knows enough to recognize a lot of the equipment he's seen so far.

Pieces of a terrifying puzzle are falling into place in Hewitt's mind, well below the surface, but reverberations from these elements are locking into place, filtering up to his surface awareness, and he doesn't like the picture those pieces are assembling.

Gale knows what they're thinking, or he assumes that they're reaching conclusions not far off from what they're thinking. He sees the changes coming over his friends as the facts start to fall into place; the tension building in Miles' shoulders, the furrowed brow of Hewitt's face, and the unfocused way Mariah is staring in his direction now that she's not following Hewitt's every move. The only ones not arriving at the same reasonable suspicion are Abraham and Ben, but that's only because they're too focused on one another. It's only a matter of time before they're all on the same page. In the cool, circulating air of the lab, Gale begins to perspire.

He distracts himself by continuing to discuss the build and the layout of the place, telling them all about the things collected within and the data they have stored securely in this location.

"Gale," Hewitt whispers, with an edge to his voice that makes everyone turn his way, "did what's happening out there come from up here?"

"Of course it did," Gale replies without any attempt at guile, distracted from what he was in the middle of saying. "I created it in this very lab."

35

—·—

CHAPTER THIRTY-FIVE

"REGARDLESS OF HOW YOU might feel about me right now, you really must appreciate the accomplishment this represents," Gale insists, his voice full of indignation. "I had to develop whole new methodologies in an effort to create something entirely novel, what you've witnessed out there."

"Well, let me be the first to say we're really fucking proud of you, doc," Mariah says. She glares at the scientist with venom and disdain. No one says anything further for a couple of minutes. Gale slumps in his seat like a scolded child, his eyes still displaying the same frustration and defiance, but he remains silent.

Finally, Hewitt speaks up. "What the fuck is it, Gale?"

"It's something new. It's something I designed myself through years of examination and careful splicing."

"That doesn't answer the question, asshole," Miles interjects tersely.

Impatiently, Gale rolls his eyes and Miles backhands him across the left side of his face for the effort. The sound of the impact jars Hewitt where he's standing and he can't help but wince.

Gale speaks up, his eyes watering. "Hewitt, you're probably the only one who's going to understand, but I'll try to keep it simple." Whether his physical reaction is the result of the slap itself or the sting of one of his oldest friends hitting him, it's difficult to tell. Everyone takes a seat at the table where the map is still spread out, eyes turned toward Gale expectantly.

"I started with illnesses that produce neurological effects like aggression and confusion or paranoia. I began approaching the problem from substrates of rabies and syphilis. That was the most difficult and time-consuming element of the process, sifting through the RNA to isolate as best I could the desired characteristics of each virus to produce the results that I was looking for. In contrast with that, the actual recombination was the very essence of simplicity.

"That isn't to say that it was simple, by any means; there was a lot of trial and error involved while I snipped and reassembled a few dozen cocktails from multiple sources. What was particularly challenging was working with animals, since I couldn't accurately gauge how it might translate into human behavior."

Gale's voice becomes more calm and clinical as he continues, explaining how he narrowed his research down to three potential candidates for the plague and couldn't get any further than that at first.

Miles slams his hand down on the table, the report of the impact stirring Gale from the almost nostalgic nature that his confession was taking. "And at no point, while you were playing mad scientist, did you stop to consider just how batshit crazy what you were doing was?"

Gale looks at him like one would a child, scoffing at the outburst but otherwise ignoring it. He begins telling his friends about how happenstance provided him with the means to pick his perfect disease.

"One of my half a dozen lab assistants made a mistake, a costly one that ultimately proved to be a fatal error," Gale continues, sounding almost somber for the first time as he recalls the details.

"We kept him in quarantine for observation while the rest of us here worked to develop some manner of treatment. He became more and more erratic and paranoid, which appeared gradual at first."

Gale abruptly sits up straight and then steps away from the table. "Actually, let me just show you something."

Gale walks to the bank of computers, drawing the attention of everyone in the room. He begins entering commands via the keyboard with a flurry so fast none of them could have hoped to replicate the keystrokes. On the large central monitor, a video begins playing, displaying a slightly overhead angled view of a middle-aged man in a white lab coat. The man is sitting on a cot in a transparent cube of a reinforced glass of some kind.

"There's no audio, I'm sorry to say. You'll understand the gist of things without it, I'm sure," Gale explains as he allows the video to tell the story for him.

The man seems uncomfortable at first, but displaying more a sort of nervous energy than anything outwardly troubling; occasionally he paces or taps his fingers on the glass in a rhythm. At times it appears that he's talking to someone out of frame but the other participant can't be seen. The time code jumps forward here and there, sometimes by hours, sometimes by a day or two. Gale had compiled this video from separate feeds to offer some manner of time-lapse.

The friends stand together, no longer able to remain seated, watching as a man devolves from human to something less as his behavior becomes angrier and even his simplest of movements or gestures carry the potential for violence. Clear degradation of mental stability is displayed as the time-lapse proceeds. No longer a man at all, it becomes impossible to consider the thing on the screen as anything other than inhuman.

Suddenly there is something more like a zombie in front of them, shuffling and shambling around, attempting to attack anyone who approaches the glass separating the former scientist from his colleagues. Attempts to feed it anything but live specimens, rodents, in particular, are only minimally successful. Raw meat appears to do the trick in place of fresh animal material, but there is a preference.

It evacuates its bowels and bladder as needed, without any attempt to contain it or remain clean, without any concession to civilization or modesty; blood and viscera stain it as well as its waste, remaining wherever it happens to fall. Finally, after three weeks of continued separation from anything that could rightly be considered human, it twitched a few times before slumping to the ground and remaining still, no longer breathing. The video ends.

"Some of them last longer," Gale speaks up, the first sound since the video had started, shocking everyone. Audible gasps can't be held back by Mariah and Abraham.

"Others don't last quite as long," he continues with the tone of a detached observer. "It's usually the improved clotting agent that does it. The same characteristic that prevents them from bleeding out from wounds that might otherwise be fatal also tends to make strokes more common. Of course, the strokes aren't always fatal and that just serves to make them seem more zombie-like in the end."

No one knows what to say. No one, aside from Gale, who has watched the video and others numerous times and who had been present for the events, just replayed at high speed for his friends. The assistant had been Gale's friend, as had the others who died along the way to what he considered the pinnacle of his life's work. Kateb had hardly been the first friend he'd lost to this plague.

"Aside from some minor tweaks, making this strain something I could package into existing vaccines, what you have on that screen is what you're seeing out there in town."

No one utters a word for a long while. Hewitt falls into his seat and holds his head between his hands, hoping to stifle the throbbing he feels. Miles appears to be on the verge of tears, displaying the same uncharacteristic emotion he'd been showing since Kateb was attacked. The others remain standing in stunned silence.

Hewitt struggles to speak, his breath catching in his throat. "What did you mean about packaging it in vaccines?"

"I'll get to that soon enough, my friend."

He continues, "It's a bit different from person to person, how quickly the subject transitions through the phases from heightened paranoia, fear, and anger to the final stage when the conscious mind is so consumed by insanity and hunger that they can't even be rightly considered human anymore. At that point, it's all about eating and spreading the sickness. The mob mentality we've seen from most of the people out there is a side-effect I should have anticipated, but it's been more than ten years since I last spent any time studying sociology. What we have out there is an amplified kin-selection drive. As the infected persons become more symptomatic, the fear and paranoia lead them to aggression directed towards anyone they perceive as being outsiders."

Mariah sighs, the look in her eyes haunted, "This could be the end of the world?"

"Nonsense," Gale responds. "This is little more than an end to the illusion of society we've been stumbling through for centuries. The plague back in the dark ages didn't end the world, and this won't either. This is where the vaccines come in. I was involved in developing and packaging vaccine shipments for delivery all over the world, in preparation for the summer flu that's on its way. I was the point man for half a dozen pharmaceutical companies, working hand-in-hand with the FDA to test and verify the quality of the vaccines before they went into mass production. It was a simple thing to slip my special cocktail into the formulas. Someone would have to be looking for it, in order to find even a trace of what I've done. For regions where flu vaccination isn't likely to be distributed, I've found ample opportunities to modify vaccine shipments for a variety of additional illnesses at home and abroad."

"Fuck you, Gale!" Miles shouts.

In response, Gale slumps a bit in the chair where he's been sitting, visibly deflating, but there's no evidence of any defeat in the tone of his voice. "You don't get it. You're going to have to adjust. Everyone has to. I've spent years now, challenging myself to leave my comfort zone, studying and practicing survivalist techniques, pushing my body past limits that I never suspected I could, and putting in literally countless hours at the gun ranges near wherever I happened to be. I've adjusted to the new world we're making here, and you will too. I've just had some lead time in getting myself prepared, and honestly, I needed it more than any of you."

"I have a wife out there, halfway across the country," Abraham mutters, the realization of just what he's been hearing fully hitting home.

"She may as well be on the moon for all the difference it seems to make right now," Hewitt says, his head still resting against his palms. The throbbing is only getting worse as he tries to concentrate on the abject lunacy he's just been listening to.

Glancing over to where his son is sleeping in the other room, exhausted from the experience of the previous days, Abraham continues with his thoughts, "Ben may never see his mother again."

Gale smiles, and everyone in the room feels ill.

"She's probably going to be fine. We'll only end up losing probably 40% of the population in the first world and 70% everywhere else, even factoring in unrelated conflicts arising from the socioeconomic impacts."

"You're talking about more than three billion people as though they're nothing," Hewitt growls. His eyes are red and his teeth are clenched. He can't disguise the rage he feels.

"This is all fucked up," Miles says. "Even as far gone as you clearly are, you have to know how positively fucked up this is."

"What it is, is necessary," Gale replies. "This is the world we have been preparing for since we were children and its the world Tristan would have thrived in instead of being ground into dust until he checked out for himself."

It amazes everyone how steady and certain Gale sounds as he says those words. The look in his eyes is pleading.

"Tristan would have never wanted something like this," Abraham says, his disgust and frustration overshadowed by disbelief and the sadness that he feels at the rationalization that he is hearing.

"The gap between what a man wants and what he needs is rarely a narrow gulf," Gale replies without a hint of shame, his gaze unwavering.

Miles slaps the table before him again, drawing all eyes his direction, "And Kateb *needed* to die for this? And what about all of those innocent people that used to live here in town? Is that all just part of what was deemed necessary in your eyes, Gale?"

Gale winces as if he's been slapped. "What happened to Kateb was an unfortunate accident, something that couldn't have been anticipated."

Mariah spins around and is unable to catch herself before the back of her hand meets Gale's face, the sound of the slap like the thunder from outside. "How can you just sit there and smugly pretend that our friend's death was an accident? You did this! You asshole! What did you expect would happen, you fucking fruitcake?"

"I did what I needed to do."

"That is a bullshit excuse," Hewitt says.

"It's not an excuse. I did this for you, for all of us certainly, but especially for you," Gale replies with indignation.

"What are you talking about?" Mariah asks, beating Hewitt to the question.

"I couldn't watch another of my friends lowered into the ground because the plastic, backward world we live in doesn't value people who are truly gifted unless they fit a rigid mold," Gale begins. "And you, my friend, are gifted like no other, in ways I can't even comprehend."

Gale refuses to look away from Hewitt's eyes as he continues, "Tristan was brilliant, no doubt, but he got bored too easily and pivoted from one thing to another until he mastered some new skill and felt the need to learn something new. As spectacular as Tristan might have been, you put that all to shame. You put us all to shame; but you have that same directionless quality, just amplified. Maybe it's undiagnosed ADHD. Maybe it's just something mixed up in the way you're wired.

"In college, you changed majors every few years, your work history can't inspire confidence in any prospective employers since they know you won't be sticking around more than a year or so, and the world has no place for icon-oclasts who don't luck into something great," Gale finally pauses to take a breath. "This won't be happening for you without something drastic changing the playing field."

Silence is the only response Hewitt can muster as he sadly shakes his head. It's overwhelming, for someone who takes responsibility seriously, hearing that the horror and devastation outside of this sheltered space is somehow be-cause of him. Intellectually, he knows that none of this is his fault but none of that alleviates the weight bearing down on him, threatening to pulp him beneath the pressure.

THERE WILL BE NO happy ending here. They all knew the reality of the situation as Gale sat there and detailed his plan. The execution was already unstoppable and the end of the world was well and truly in progress. There was no way to bring all of this to a halt. He'd set it up so that it would all proceed as planned, whether he was still alive or not.

Even with a vaccine or any sort of treatment that could mitigate the spread of this new disease, neither of which existed if Gale could be believed, the effects could dev-astate society across the globe, and nothing would ever be the same, especially in the civilized world. There is no salvaging this situation from what Hewitt can see. Gale had fundamentally eroded any sense of camaraderie or even familiarity his friends felt toward him up until this point.

The revelations have them all reeling, but Hewitt feels like the rug has been pulled from under his feet, yanking reality with it, and he is left tumbling into a vast abyss where the floor should have been. The responsibility for this tragic and horrific series of events has been thrust upon him and the burden threatens to crush him. He recognizes the mental gymnastics required to treat this situation as if it's somehow his fault and momentarily he hates Gale even more for this; because he can follow the reasoning, he can't even help but wonder if maybe his friend was right.

Maybe he was following the same path Tristan had a few years before. He was just slower in arriving at the same terminal destination. It wasn't like he hadn't considered it in the past. Being honest with himself, it was a more common thought than he would have admitted to any of his friends, including Mariah.

Hewitt certainly seemed to have never really found his place in the world. Gale was right in that assessment; Tristan had always been Hewitt's companion in that particular boat. He finds himself hating Gale a little more, knowing that there is no reason for him to be taking any of this on his shoulders. He glares over at Gale and his former friend looks away. Sheepish, over in the corner, Gale stares at the floor.

He feels no shame for what he's done, and the sullen, chastised expression has everything to do with the reaction from his friends rather than any awareness of how wrong he was. He had been so entrenched in believing he was doing the right thing that he expected them all to understand the same thing. The numerous attempts at rationalizing and justifying his actions while he ranted on and on about how much work he'd put into all of this, the grim details of test after test and the deaths of his various assistants, finally explaining why the lab was empty when they arrived.

It had gone on for what seemed like hours, Gale proudly sharing his greatest accomplishment with the people he expected to appreciate it most. He'd brought their zombie movies to life, he'd made their childhood fantasies true, and he sincerely believed they would thank him for it. Mariah has to admit to herself that maybe there's some truth in Gale's belief that Tristan would've thrived in the environment their friend has worked so diligently to create. But it doesn't make anything about what he's done, right.

The diatribe continued, wearing them all down and draining them of any sense of reality until Miles hit him and Gale finally shut up. The blow from Miles seemed to have rocked him to the core in a way he'd been unprepared to absorb. There is already some swelling and bruising appearing on his lips and cheek.

Miles wants to hit him again, and he's grateful for the discipline he's had hammered into him over the years. He keeps reliving those final moments of Kateb's life, and the pain and confusion on his friend's face haunts him. He was always close to every one of these people, but what he felt toward Kateb and how they had bonded, it was something deeper and more meaningful. All of that is gone, just like that, relegated to only memories.

It was meaningless, all of this. More importantly, in Miles' eyes, it was intentional and malicious; worse than that, it was caused by someone he believed to be a friend. Miles knows that he will never be able to reconcile with Gale. He wants to hit him and keep hitting him until there is nothing left but pulp. He is entirely certain that he is going to feel this same way tomorrow and for probably every day of the rest of his life.

Abraham is too stunned by everything to react. The shit Gale had put Ben through by bringing this nightmare to life made him want to hurt the lunatic. He had been almost satisfied when Miles had punched him instead. His son had witnessed things Abraham never would have imagined, and there would be no recovering after this. These experiences are going to be a source of trauma all through Ben's life. He is sure of that.

Ben had taken it all well, but his father is sure that shock plays some part in that. Once there has been time to breathe and reflect, the impact can be evaluated.

36

CHAPTER THIRTY-SIX

HEWITT KNEELS IN FRONT of the man they once considered one of their best friends. There is madness in Gale's eyes as he visibly bounces between indignation and despair. Hewitt can't wrap his head around the apparent logic motivating a crime this awful, but he doesn't doubt that Gale had good intentions somewhere in the twisted corridors of his mind. The man he knows would need some reasonable basis upon which this absolute horror had been assembled. He still can't accept that this was somehow because of him though, that's simply a bridge too far.

"Buddy, you have got to give me something here. I need you to tell me how to stop this," Hewitt pleads.

Gale inhales deeply and sighs, finally focusing his eyes on the friend directly in front of him as if he's seeing him there for the first time. "There is no stopping it anymore. The time to do that was already gone before you guys even arrived here. That was part of the reason I even invited you all, to keep you out of the way of this." He sighs again, his shoulders dropping as he exhales, "I did this to keep you safe."

"Look around you, Gale. Take a serious look around. None of us are safe here. We're fucking lucky Kateb is the only one who didn't make it here to this great concrete fucking tomb of yours. There's some cruel irony in that being the case."

Gale flinches at the mention of Kateb, and his eyes are moist, but there are no tears. "There is no turning back the clock for the infected, Hewitt," he replies, for the first time sounding even a little forlorn. "There are bound to be people out there who might be immune to this, but it's not likely. What with the viral scaffold I used being rabies. I may have borrowed from assorted other viral sources and bacteria to get the final product, but at the core, the rabies virus is the delivery package. I really did try to develop a vaccine with that in mind, modifying the existing rabies vaccinations with the new pathogen, but I'd changed the disease too much and never made any discernible progress."

"You could still do it," Hewitt suggests.

Gale looks around the room, meeting every set of eyes with his own before he speaks again. "I'm not crazy, you know? Despite what you all seem to think, I'm not crazy. The plan was to have you all inoculated before the release, but I just couldn't work it out. The next best thing I could do was to get you all here where you might be able to acclimate yourselves to the new world in my test run here. I figured that would get you ready for the world beyond this valley. No one was supposed to get hurt. Kateb wasn't supposed to die!"

The passion in Gale's voice transforms to anguish by the end, and tears are visible trailing down his cheeks.

"There is no cure though," he says after a minute. "I wasn't smart enough to develop one, or maybe I was too close to it all to see what I might have been overlooking." He pauses before locking eyes with Hewitt and patting his friend on the shoulder reassuringly. "You're welcome to check my work. Every bit of research is thoroughly documented here, disconnected from any external networks. Maybe you'll see something I didn't, but even as smart as you are, I think maybe I just outdid myself with this."

He tries to smile, and it's the saddest thing Hewitt's seen, the reality of what he's done seems finally to have gotten through his barriers of arrogance and righteousness and there is nothing he can think of that justifies a smile at this point. Hewitt gives up, lifting himself to his feet and drifting away to one of the rooms meant for the absent staff to sleep up here at the top level of the facility.

As he enters the room, he tries not to imagine himself standing atop a teeming mass of sickness and plague like the king of some pestilential mountain. He drops heavily onto the glorified cot and falls quickly asleep, letting exhaustion ferry him across the divide and into oblivion.

THERE IS ONLY SILENCE in the cavernous space after Hewitt walks away. No one has anything further to say, and no one wants to listen to anything else for fear that their world might be further shattered by new revelations. Emotionally drained and worn as thin as she thinks she can ever be without snapping like a twig, Mariah follows Hewitt to bed only a few minutes later, finding him already asleep.

Devastated and reeling from everything they've heard, the others aren't far behind. Abraham finds himself secretly hoping that if he just goes to sleep, he can wake up and find that all of this has been nothing more than some awful nightmare. He knows it's a childish fantasy and that it's an escapist mentality to even entertain such thoughts, but he makes the wish just the same.

Miles finally walks away, casting one final glance over his shoulder at Gale as he retires to a room of his own. Gale can't properly read the look, but it isn't hatred so much as disappointment and it isn't fear as much as disgust.

37

CHAPTER THIRTY-SEVEN

GALE IS LEFT ALONE, the only one still awake and intent on remaining so. He is moderately surprised that Miles hadn't tied him up or bound him in some fashion before retiring for the night. Even so, he doesn't move from his seat for more than half an hour; the time spent staring blankly ahead with an expression on his face that any of his friends would recognize. He had always lapsed into this same expression when the gears were turning behind his eyes and his thoughts became so frenzied that he lost track of the world outside and became enmeshed within his mind.

When he finally does move from the chair, he doesn't go far. Seated in front of the main computer terminal, he opens a series of windows and his fingers type furiously away at the keys for nearly an hour before he glances over the product of his labor with grim satisfaction.

Gale stands and walks around this upper level of the facility, checking in on his sleeping friends and retrieving various entry cards from a locked drawer before labeling them and placing them on the desk before the terminal where he'd been working. From another locked drawer, Gale retrieves a Glock 9mm handgun, and he leaves through the front door. No one hears him pass through the airlock on his way out.

At the entrance to the mine itself, he sits on the gravel, gazing out over the forested distance, recalling the fighting that took place over the last few hours and the disappointment of his friends. For the first time since he started down this path so many years before, he actively wonders if he was wrong, but knows that it doesn't matter anymore. They will never forgive him either way, and there's nothing he can do to change the events he'd set in motion.

Tristan and Kateb were gone, and illogical as the thinking might be, Gale feels at fault for both deaths. He doesn't feel guilty about the innumerable deaths he's responsible for with this new plague of his devising, but he can't avoid how he's feeling about the friends he failed to save. He's done what he can, though. He's given his remaining friends everything he can to make sure they stay alive. There's no guarantee they'll survive what's coming, but he's played his part. He gave them the information they'll need.

He's no longer necessary. His presence is no longer wanted, and he understands why. He wishes they could understand his reasoning, but maybe they will in time. No one inside hears the gunshot and, in the town below, the echo reverberates across the valley as little more than a pop, its origin lost to anyone who might have been listening at the time to hear it. Gale slumps to the ground in the faint light from a sun struggling to penetrate the thick cloud cover with even feeble illumination.

***

MILES IS THE FIRST awake. Discipline from years of pre-dawn maneuvers and activity never fades away. He walks the perimeter of the large interior space, checking in on his still-sleeping friends and noticing that Gale is nowhere to be found.

He considers the possibility that the nut job had ventured deeper down into the facility, but tells himself that he can't imagine why. In reality, he can imagine numerous reasons for Gale doing so, but none of them are good and they all pile horror upon horror and he doesn't want to think about those things. He's given up on trying to understand Gale's motives though, and nothing much would surprise him at this point.

He sincerely believed that nothing would surprise him. The monochromatic display being fed by the security cameras pauses on an image that manages to surprise him. It shakes him to the foundation of his being. The view has changed again before he's even had a chance to process what he'd seen and he remains there, unmoving, while he waits for the feed to cycle back through again.

The image returns and Miles sits hard in the chair behind him, hardly noticing that he's moved at all. The camera feed keeps on cycling through the various angles and locations and each time it returns to that image of Gale, he unconsciously swallows and releases a breath he hasn't noticed he'd been holding in.

He is still in the same position, unaware that he is quietly crying, when Hewitt pads sleepily up behind him an hour later. Seeing the same heartbreaking image for himself, he silently puts his arm around Miles' shoulder and Miles reaches up to grab it with his own hand. The feed continues cycling and Hewitt joins him in shedding tears for another wasted life.

38

CHAPTER THIRTY-EIGHT

STILL REELING FROM THE horrifying revelations, having finally had a chance to process the loss of Kateb and the horrifying sequence of events that followed, Hewitt stands at the entrance to the Mine, staring into the night. Reflected on the low-hanging clouds, he can see the impressions of the few lights still shedding their glow on the streets below that are out of sight through the trees. From the distance, he could fool himself into believing there's a place of sanctuary and life down there. He knows there's nothing to be found there but death.

"It's only a matter of time before the more lucid members of that mob think about the mine and come for us here," he mutters as Mariah approaches and stands at his side. "They will remember this place exists and those fuckers, whatever we call them, will think to search for outsiders up here."

"Maybe they're already too far gone for that," she replies. "Gale said that the progression from the early stages to final expression is pretty rapid."

Fingers curl together as they take each other's hands.

"He also said that it varies considerably." Hewitt pauses to look up at the sky. The thick clouds he knows are up there, hidden by the darkness. "But this rain isn't going to last forever and the floodwaters are going to recede. Nothing will stop these monsters from getting out of here and spreading."

"You heard Gale. By now, this same thing is happening in every corner of every civilized nation as well as most of the places we wouldn't think of as civilized." Mariah pauses as she inhales a shuddering breath. "We've lost. Any of them that shuffle their way out of here are hardly going to be a drop in the bucket."

He turns to her, tears welling up in his eyes. "We still have to fight. Every one of them that we stop could mean dozens of lives saved."

Mariah releases his hand, wraps her arm around his waist, and whispers, "No matter what Gale said to rationalize this shit, this is not your fault."

The embrace lasts only a few seconds before she lets him go and retreats to the interior of the mine, where their friends are still sorting through the facts and looking through the lab. She knows that her presence won't help Hewitt right now and that he'll need to process everything on his own. She joins Miles and Abraham, where they are digging through paperwork, trying to decipher Gale's notes. So far, there's been nothing that points to a cure or any way of stopping the plan he's implemented. Exhausted, mortified, and in shock, they can't help but try to find a solution.

No one realizes how much time has passed when Hewitt returns to the lab, wiping his eyes as he exits the darkness of the mine and crosses into the stark contrast of the room. They all look up as they hear him come in. His voice is steadier than he feels, by far, "We need to go on the offensive here. We have to start here and we have to act quickly."

As he speaks he feels a sense of calm descending over him. "This may be a losing battle and the world may just be ending, at least the world as we know it. If we can make even a small difference in how this all plays out, we have to try."

Hewitt replays the words in his head, feeling like a third-rate actor in a B-movie, spouting off some inspirational, poorly scripted, delusional dialogue that's supposed to serve as a rousing speech.

"Cue the musical score, poorly imitating Williams. This is where it reaches a crescendo," Hewitt mutters to himself, loud enough for his friends to hear him.

Miles and Mariah both start laughing and Miles crosses the distance to his friend, wrapping his huge arms around him, squeezing too tightly for comfort.

"You're right, brother," he says.

"Mariah, you were right too," Hewitt says after taking a moment to catch his breath. "This may only be a drop in the bucket, but it could be that single drop that breaks the surface tension and causes everything to spill over the edge of that bucket. It could be the final drop that strains the dam. We may not be able to make much of a dent, but even a small chance of that seems like a good enough reason to get active here."

He takes another deep breath, looking from one friend's eyes to another. "Besides, if this is the apocalypse, we should clear out this fucking place so that there's a haven of some kind. We're isolated up here, with only one effective way in or out, and honestly, no one knows this town exists. If I were going to plan a place to rebuild from, this wouldn't be too far off from ideal. We aren't far from Spokane or even Missoula in the other direction, and there are numerous smaller towns dotting the region. Supply runs from here and recovery of survivors to somewhere safe and sheltered could be managed from here. I know it seems crazy, but this place is about fucking perfect."

Miles is quiet while he mulls over his friend's words.

When he finally speaks, it's with an analytical tone, "Hewitt's right. If we can sweep this town and keep it intact in the process, this place could be a good jumping-off point to everywhere west of the Rockies. This place is maybe six hours from Seattle, less than that from Boise. There are going to be survivors all over the place, people who didn't get the tainted vaccines and who managed to avoid being slaughtered. There are definitely going to be plenty of supplies. Even if everything has already gone to shit out there, and I'm not sure that it has, we can't just hide out here in a cave while we wait for the road to clear out, leaving these fuckers to our rear."

Heads begin to nod all around the room. Abraham looks down at his son before responding, "There could be some uninfected people still here in town as well, as unlikely as that seems. The deputy certainly was. The odds might be slim, based on what we've seen, but we can't know for sure unless we act here and now.

IT'S WET AND GLOOMY as the five of them gaze down at the mostly darkened town with only the first faint hints of dawn brightening the sky behind the mountains to the East. From the high vantage point, they can make out the occasional flashlight or lantern as the residents who still have some of their faculties scurry about, probably searching for the outsiders who are right now cataloging the movements.

The rain has temporarily died down, but they all know it can pick up again at any time and none of them are sure which will be better for what is coming.

Miles is nominally in charge of their group at this point; his years of combat experience and familiarity with conflict of a sort similar to what they are all anticipating with varying degrees of fear and apprehension. Miles had committed the map to memory while he was inside and he is seeing it overplayed on the scene stretching out before him. The map was all fine and good but it neglected too many details of the terrain and the overall environment. He may not have been the intellectual equal of some of his friends, but this is his wheelhouse.

He reaches over and pats Hewitt on the upper arm before gesturing back to the direction of the mine entrance. Hewitt nods and gets the attention of the others. Back in the dryer confines of the lab, Miles gazes down at the map from the same angle they had from the hill outside. After a few minutes, he begins sketching out symbols representative of trees, hedges, sheds, and other items not appearing on the map. Miles looks up, apparently satisfied with the small number of updates he's made, indicated by a grunt-like sound he makes unconsciously as he evaluates and reviews it.

"Is there anything else you guys want to add? Anything you recall from your time down there?" Miles asks. "Close your eyes for a minute or two and try to visualize everything you recall and see if you can locate it on the map."

Ben jumps up from his seat, gesturing to his father that he should come with him. The two make some notations together after spending a short while conferring about it and discussing their attempted retreat to Gale's house only a couple of nights before. It isn't much, but it's more than they had. Mariah and Hewitt each take turns making their own additions to the map. After they've all finished, the unfolded paper is hardly similar to its original appearance.

Hewitt has to admit to himself that it does look a lot more like what they'd seen from above with the alterations in place. It's hardly perfect and what they could pick up from above in the dark was limited.

"There's not going to be any more of that splitting up bullshit when we go back out there," Miles says, laughing. "You know, to cover more ground like we've all seen in movies. That shit is only for Hollywood."

Every set of eyes is on him and all of them nod in response, a couple of them even smiling.

"Even if we had twice our number, that wouldn't be an option under these circumstances," Miles continues, his tone suddenly more serious.

"That sounds fine to me," Hewitt replies.

"Same here," says Abraham.

"You are staying up here, kid," Miles says, pointing to Ben. "I know you're a bright kid and you can handle yourself just fine. Look at what you went through with your old man just to get here. You and the old man made it through hell the other night, no doubt about that, but shit is going to get real ugly down there and we need your dad focused on what's directly in front of him and not worrying about you."

Ben looks like he's planning to argue for a few seconds before he sits back in a slump, nodding his head. "I understand."

The planning begins in earnest.

Miles plots a route skirting the town as best they can to get back to Gale's house, where more of his firearms are locked in the hidden compartment at the rear of his SUV. What they have on them isn't going to be enough for the clean-up Miles has in mind. It's already afternoon by the time they finish going over preparations and since they have a busy night ahead of them, they all attempt to sleep. Fitfully and sporadically, they do finally sleep.

39

— · —

Chapter Thirty-Nine

As NIGHT APPROACHES, THEY fortify themselves as well as they can and Ben shuts himself away in a room he can lock from the inside. Slowly, the four friends navigate the wet hillside, staying to the side of the gravel road to remain hidden in case someone happens to be watching. Miles' precautions may have seemed paranoid on the surface, but none of the rest of them felt like they should argue.

They venture from the road where Miles indicates they should and they venture more slowly through the forested area, leaving the road to their back. As they approach the first house along the way, they halt in the thick brush just beyond the yard and form a huddle.

"Guns are our last resort here," Hewitt reminds everyone.

Miles nods. "The last thing we want is to be drawing any attention when we're not ready for it, and right now we are not outfitted to be drawing any unwanted attention. Those fuckers will tear us apart if we get swarmed."

They cross the lawn as quickly and quietly as they can. The rear door handle doesn't move when Abraham tries it and they move on to the side entrance near the driveway. That handle turns without any difficulty.

Starting with the first floor, they check each room with low-light LED flashlights Miles had picked up from his car before heading to the mine before he realized everything was well and truly gone to shit. The faint, red illumination makes it seem like their surroundings are coated in a film of blood. Hewitt can't help but consider how appropriate that is.

The first house is thankfully empty and they continue. Skirting the scattered homes on the outskirts of town, they manage to travel a good distance before reaching the trailer that serves as the next space needing to be swept. Neither the front nor back door is open, and Miles is forced to kick the back door in, splintering the frame away from the wall in the process.

Mariah steps in first, buffeted by the coppery scent of blood, sweeping the living room with the eerie red light as the others enter swiftly behind her. Wood and glass curio cabinets showcase dozens of Hummel figurines and the rest of the decor isn't any more tasteful. *It's like some unsettling, horror movie tribute to grandmothers everywhere*, she thinks as she follows the path of the light over the interior of the trailer.

Hewitt steps through the door just as the light sweeps over a man sprawled out on the plastic-covered sofa. They sweep their lights over the same man multiple times before he registers this presence. Hewitt visibly starts as he realizes the man is there and that his wide-open eyes are staring directly at them without blinking. The massive wound on his neck isn't as obvious right away when everything is already red.

It's clear to all of them that the man isn't breathing before they get very close and, with the extent of the damage to his throat, it comes as no surprise to any of them. Violating the silence of the trailer, they hear the sound of thumping and scratching as it arises from their left, down a darkened hallway. Cautiously, Miles takes the lead down the hall, hefting the fire axe in preparation.

It isn't difficult to locate the source of the increasingly frantic noise. The cheap door rattles against the frame, ever so slightly bulging near the center as each new thud occurs. A substantially more sturdy wooden chair braces the door closed. No one is eager to remove the obstruction, likely put in place by the dead man in the living room sometime before he died from his injury. There is no shock and no surprise. They all know what they are going to find behind that door.

The only thing up in the air is who it might be lurking there and struggling to get out. It's sure to be a spouse, a child, or a parent of the dead man in the living room, someone he would have had in his home close enough to injure him and not be killed immediately in response.

The smell is awful with the door shut; it becomes progressively more potent as they approach; a miasma of waste and sickness seems to pervade the air all around them. It is the odor of a new sort of death, one even Miles isn't inured to. When Miles kicks the chair out of the way and the door comes crashing open, he is almost too sickened by the sight and smell to swing the axe down at the neck of the bloated, naked, old woman who burst through the open space, falling to the ground without the door to support her.

Hesitation aside, when the swing does connect, it hits true and the spine at the base of her skull is severed with a crunch that makes Hewitt cringe. None of them will forget that sound combined with the scent, even if they live longer lives than any of them believe to be likely in the present surroundings.

Everyone is relieved to be back out in the rain once they finish clearing the house. The smell only seemed to get worse the longer they spent inside until it felt like it would never go away, following them for the rest of their days. It was the sort of thing that seemed like it might contaminate them, seeping into their pores to remain with them.

The next couple of properties they explore are comparatively uneventful. It isn't until the final house before they are expecting to approach the rear of Gale's property that they are greeted with the same terrible odor. Miles holds up his hand to stop them, concerned that they are picking up the scent as far away as the line of trees before the lawn begins.

Peering through the night, he can see that one window on the main floor is shattered, but that doesn't explain the smell being so potent at this distance. Crouching down, Miles begins to skirt alongside the foliage, attempting to obtain a different view of the home. Taking his cue, the others shrink down as best they can manage.

Abraham's voice erupts in a sound somewhere between a scream and a grunt, as he tries to muffle the noise with his hand immediately as it begins. Hewitt switches on his flashlight, swinging it toward Abraham, only to see an emaciated, infected man gripping his friend's pant leg and ripping into the side of his shin with broken, gnashing teeth. The flesh of Abraham's leg is abraded as the teeth graze against bone and slide along the surface.

It's a sight only available for a moment before the thicker end of a baseball bat hammers into the thing's head, dislodging it from Abraham's leg. Another downward blow follows the first, like a piston descending, stopping the man dead just as Miles makes it back from his interrupted search around the perimeter. They rush into the house with less caution than they would have exhibited only minutes earlier, and they lay Abraham down on a loveseat in the living room.

Miles begins examining his friend's wound while Hewitt and Mariah sweep the house for any remaining danger, disregarding the earlier insistence that there would be no splitting up. With tears in his eyes, Abraham knows what the injury means. They all know. Gale had made it clear, perfectly clear, what the outcome would be with this sort of direct exposure.

The bite itself isn't bad. Bone stopped the teeth from digging too deeply. Miles figures his friend may not even have a limp while they finish out their mission, but the damaged denim and broken skin foretold something much worse than a limp. Hewitt and Mariah return to the den just as Miles is finished bandaging the wound. There is no time for commiseration. They are almost where they need to be.

They arrive at Gale's house with no further excitement and nothing appears to have been touched. The other three change into warmer, dry clothing from their luggage while Miles digs through his SUV. Even Abraham looks happier when he returns to the dining room seeing the firearms laid out on the table, almost happy enough to push the thoughts of the infection surely coursing through his veins from his mind.

40

CHAPTER FORTY

ABRAHAM BEGAN COLLEGE IMMEDIATELY out of high school, choosing not to travel far from home, content to remain close to his family. After almost four years of studying civil engineering with a minor in materials, Abraham changed tracks and shifted his focus to architecture, having fallen in love with some of the buildings right there on campus. During the summer months, he worked in construction, doing everything from carpentry to bricklaying and concrete, and he applied his education to the practical experience he was dealing with regularly.

He realized that he wanted to do more while he was watching those buildings take shape before his eyes, to leave his mark, and repairing infrastructure wasn't going to be sufficient for him. He was going to make a name for himself by designing homes and businesses, not bridges or roadways. With his contacts in construction, he believed he could leverage an architecture degree and experience in running his own firm. It was a lofty goal; he knew it, but he believed it was something he could pull off if he played his cards right.

It took him longer than he wanted, but after only three years working as an apprentice, Abraham finally got his chance. It was as much luck as anything else. While he'd been in college, working toward his original plan of a degree in civil engineering, he met the woman of his dreams and it just so happened that, seven years later, she was instrumental in helping him bring his dreams to life.

Over the Christmas holiday with her family, he was introduced to an uncle who was looking to avoid renewing a lease on the commercial property his business operated from and he wanted to build something to his specifications, somewhere he could guarantee that the infrastructure was suitable for his needs. Abraham felt the man out for details, trying to keep the conversation casual, and spent the rest of the holiday vacation working on a draft for the building.

The proposal was a hit, and the money was enough for him to break out on his own. With his wife handling the finances and secretarial work during those early days, and Abraham cultivating a network from his connections on the job and former classmates, they began their own contracting and architectural firm. The first few years after starting up were a bit rough and taxing, especially with a small child in tow around the office, but once they started making a name for themselves, the work took off.

The firm grew, and they cemented themselves as being the firm businesses and individuals could turn to in order to address issues other architects refused to tackle. Abraham's background in civil engineering and materials made it possible for him to look at problems of logistics and environment from different angles than a lot of his competition, not being mired in traditional forms and solutions. Over time, his work ethic and unwillingness to take home more profit than he needed allowed him to retain loyal staff and undercut his contemporaries in many cases.

During the early years of running his own business, he and his family lived a fairly spartan lifestyle, though they never had to want for anything. Abraham and his wife agreed that it was best to invest much of what they would have been taking home back into the business.

By the time he and Ben began their journey to Idaho, Abraham's firm had contracts all over the United States and Canada, largely commercial interests but also a great many residential projects, being managed mostly by his wife while he and the boy went away on this vacation. His family had moved into a new home only a year before, a home he'd designed as a proof of concept. The years of reinvestment in his company had built them a business that could run itself while Abraham was away, something he was pleased to know, just as he knew his wife was mostly just enjoying the time away from a house full of men.

His wife regularly teased him that he could retire early if he kept running the business the way he had. That was something he'd never do, and she knew him well enough to know that much, too. He loved his work too much, and he loved that he had built something with his wife as a partner that could carry on for generations if Ben grew up wanting to follow in his father's footsteps.

Ben knew how to read blueprints almost as early as he could read children's books and the countless hours spent sitting on his father's lap in the office had embedded the sounds of graphite on paper into his young mind as something integral to happiness.

41

CHAPTER FORTY-ONE

THE MAP IS UNFOLDED, and spread out over the coffee table in Gale's den. Miles has marked the houses they already secured on their route from the lab to where they've been relaxing for the last hour. The blinds are all drawn tight to cut down on any risk of someone seeing the light through the storm, still stubbornly carrying on outside.

"We don't know whether these locations will remain secure," Miles suggests as he gestures toward the residences he's marked off with a red X. "The population out there is moving around a bit, but they still seem to be returning to their respective homes to sleep and so on, at least the ones still human enough to give a shit about that sort of thing."

"So, the odds are an even split that we could have problems from the places we believe we've already dealt with?" Hewitt asks.

"As far as the more human among the infected? Yes."

"What about the zombies?" Mariah asks.

Miles thinks for a moment. "I have no fucking clue. Those things are altogether inhuman."

"Well, we do have one thing in our favor," Mariah points out. "The thinking and unthinking amongst our enemies out there are as prone to attack and kill each other as they are any of us."

"There is that," Hewitt replies, trying to look on the bright side and to wrap his head around the fact that this was suddenly the bright side.

"It's a small consolation that's going to be for us once we're out there again," Miles says. "I've been in the middle of multiple hostile parties who are just as unfriendly toward one another as they were our own forces. It just adds another layer of disorientation to an already confusing situation and makes it imperative that we all remain alert and watch all sides."

Mariah sighs, "At least here is some depletion in the numbers, for both sides, because of that conflict. There was previously a population of twelve hundred out there, with what, five hundred homes, give or take a dozen or so? Those are nightmare logistics by anyone's standards."

Abraham adds, "She's right about that. Out of these twelve hundred people, we can only legitimately account for maybe two or three dozen dead. That's a drop in the bucket unless they've thinned out their own numbers quite a bit and, forgive me for saying it, I fucking hope they have been busy doing precisely that."

Hewitt nods and a moment later, so does Miles.

"We haven't got ammunition for an all-out assault against that sort of force," Miles agrees. "We have to be smart about this and employ a bit of strategy."

Hewitt replies, "Even as careful as we might be, some of these people can easily slip past us unseen. Some of them probably already have."

"Gale said that bit about fear of outsiders and I am pinning some hope on that aspect of the sickness, keeping them in familiar locations. I could be wrong, but it's about all I have to be optimistic about."

"That's a pretty big fucking 'if' hanging over our heads, buddy," Hewitt says.

"It is," Mariah adds after a pause.

"Hey, it's all we have. It's the only thing that might be working in our favor to contain the infected here," Miles responds. They all stand in silence for a minute before they continue sorting through firearms and ammunition in defeated silence. With the first slight hints of sunrise behind the thick cloud cover, the group gives in to their exhaustion and they decide to sleep in shifts until night.

The work they have ahead of them, they all agree, is the sort of thing best kept to the shadows.

As well as they'd tried to clean and treat the wound, Abraham developed a fever while he was sleeping. It's mild, but it's disheartening. Intellectually, they had known how this would work out, but they'd all hoped Abraham would, by some miracle, avoid the infection in a way none of the locals had.

"I'm ok," he insists. "Just a little bit warm and there's a little bit of pressure behind my eyes right now."

"We can get you back to Ben," Mariah suggests, "before we get started on this."

"Absolutely not!" he replies.

"As much as one extra set of eyes and a couple of trigger fingers will help out," Miles says, as soothing as any of them had heard him be, "It's ok for you to spend this time with your son."

Abraham sighs. "You don't get it. Ben doesn't need to see me like this and I don't want to risk hurting him somehow when this progresses further. None of us know how long I will actually be me."

There is no disagreeing with him and Hewitt thinks it all through, realizing that there is no argument to be made. It is a sound decision and they are going to need every possible set of eyes out there.

Loaded up, no further discussion to be had, they set out into the night. Mirroring Miles as best they can, they appear almost professional in their coordination. Alley to alley, yard to yard, the four of them keeping to the shadows, they cover a lot of ground quickly.

Navigating their way along the opposite edge of town from the path they'd taken to get to Gale's, they run into no real trouble. More people are found dead in their homes. What's troubling more than anything is how many of those who should have been dead they're finding, both indoors and out.

Unexpectedly for everyone but Miles, the challenge comes in dispatching sleeping people. Feverish and sweating, in the throes of nightmares, it is clear they are infected. Murdering people in their sleep is something sure to haunt them all. Mariah, for a moment, finds herself envious of the fact that Abraham won't be carrying these memories around with him as long as the rest of them presumably will.

These thoughts come to her, unbidden, immediately after standing over an elderly woman and driving the blade of a machete through her sternum and into her heart. She wakes momentarily but makes no sound and dies without a fight. Some of the sleeping infected put up more of a fight than others, but the only time they need to fire a round is when Miles puts down one of the townsfolk who had turned into a zombie, trapped inside of their home.

Hewitt stares in horror while Miles stands there with the barrel leveled at the thing shuffling towards him. He almost raises his gun when lightning lights up the sky and Miles fires just as the thunder shakes the air. Tapping his friend gently on the shoulder, Hewitt gestures applause when Miles looks back at him. Miles chuckles quietly, the sound lost in the rain.

Time is funny for them. To Hewitt, it seems like the process of sweeping the new edge of the town has taken forever by the time they work their way back to the route up the hill and to the mine. The whole thing had taken less than two hours. There is still plenty of time left for them to continue with the gruesome chore.

42

— · —

CHAPTER FORTY-TWO

Miles' plan is still the same, to start from the side of the town nearest the lab and to clear everything moving outward from there. It makes sense to everyone, creating a distance between the infected and the one place they desperately want to keep secure. It is a blessing that the population had remained unaware that the mine might still be used for something. They want to be sure to minimize any risk of that detail changing, especially with Ben in hiding up there.

Sweeping the homes becomes a simple routine but far more risky as they reach the point where the streets and houses begin to take on a more traditional city block lay-out. In these areas, they also have to contend with the emergency-powered street lamps that are painting the environment with their haunting, orange-red glow. Moving from home to home is faster, by far, but the chance of being caught out in the open or being heard is substantially increased.

Miles had warned them that they were going to start feeling greater tension, where population density was sure to be higher. All of these windows and adjoining lawns filled with shadows could easily be playing host to any number of unseen threats. The same things they utilize to their benefit could easily be turned against them. Unlike anyone infected who might simply be lurking about, the four friends must remain on the move, exposing themselves, no matter how hard they work to remain hidden.

"These are the experiences that stick with you, haunt you," Miles had said. "This shit, right here, what you'll be going through tonight is the kind of horror that builds up PTSD in trained soldiers."

Only halfway through the night, they all understand the truth of Miles' warning. Every sound is a new threat. The rain and thunder mask dangers from their senses. Behind every darkened window are murderous, leering faces just waiting for them to break in. Every shadow harbors a monster primed to lurch out and devour them.

This is fucking exhausting, Abraham thinks to himself. On top of the strain of knowing what awaits him as the disease takes greater hold, he is feeling worse than when the night had started. He simply doesn't have the energy to cope with all the added stress.

He is terrified he might slip up somehow, and turn on his friends or, god forbid, his son. The hours of awful, strenuous labor take a toll on them all. Even Miles, as accustomed to violence and grueling conditions as he is, never experienced anything quite so horrifying.

They never know what they'll be walking into from one house to the next. Some of the places resemble slaughterhouse killing floors and others are so pristine that it feels like they've stepped into an episode of The Twilight Zone. Sometimes these two types of homes are right next door to one another.

Only an hour before dawn, they have successfully infiltrated and cleared thirty homes with fewer than twenty rounds fired between all the firearms they carry with them. The work itself was terrible, but it went smoother than any of them expected. One more house on this block before they can look forward to returning to the lab and resting until the next evening. Abraham is relieved more than any of them. He has been slowing down.

"I'm going to stick around out here on the porch to keep watch," he says, his voice faint and hoarse.

After a few moments of consideration, Miles nods, and both Hewitt and Mariah follow suit.

"Take a break, buddy," he says. "We'll be out quickly."

The house is empty and quiet. Even taking their time to be diligent in their search, they are out quickly. Back on the porch, they find only an empty seat where their friend had been sitting. Hewitt is the one who notices the blood, but it's Mariah who hears the inarticulate voices and the faint sounds of struggle just around the corner. They move as swiftly as they can, only to catch a glimpse of three people hauling a man they know is Abraham down the next block, his form slumped and being dragged rather than carried.

Carefully, the three of them follow as close as they dare, venturing into a section of town they hadn't cleared yet and weren't planning to address until the following night. They know they are heading toward the town square and public park. They were all familiar with that location and what has been going on there. Even in a disoriented state and being dragged along, Abraham recognizes the path he is being taken along. He knows where this journey will end.

Fueled by equal parts fever and terror, he struggles so much that he receives a solid blow to his temple as a reward. He doesn't lose consciousness, but he loses his fight. Abraham goes limp and dazed, head slumping as the sound of frenzied groans and rumblings begins to rise over the sound of the rain and his own body dragging roughly against the pavement. It's all so familiar, like Deja vu.

Maybe it's the fever or the probable concussion, but he finds himself drifting back and forth between memory and the present situation. Is any of this real or is he still wandering through town with Ben, making their slow progress toward Gale's house? As he is dragged into the park, surrounded by rabid townsfolk, Abraham continues along in the fugue state, and it is a blessing as he is kicked, jabbed at cruelly, and pelted with rocks of various sizes on his path through the gauntlet.

His friends stop short, knowing now why they'd run into so few people in their homes. Clearly, most of the population who hadn't crossed over into that final, feral stage of the sickness are right here in the town square. Through the rain, it is impossible to make an accurate headcount, but more than half of the town's residents appear to be milling about in the park.

Hidden, deep in shadows, they watch as their friend is led through the crowd toward the newly erected stake in the center. They all recall his and Ben's account of what had happened in this place only a couple of days earlier and probably every night since then. These people are active nocturnally, probably sleeping during the day, those who could still sleep at least. Judging by what they'd seen, hardly anyone was sleeping anymore, a symptom that is steadily pushing their lunacy further.

"We can't get him out of there," Hewitt says, his tone panicked and despondent.

"No chance," Miles confirms. They watch, feeling helpless, as Abraham is dragged closer to the giant stake jutting up from the center of the crowd.

"We have one thing we can do," Miles says suddenly, feeling hollow inside as the words leave his mouth. "We can grant him some mercy, something those fuckers will never do."

Hewitt and Mariah are quick to understand what he's saying, but neither of them knows what to say. Hewitt knows he can't disagree with the cold logic of the suggestion or the compassion.

"Mariah's the best shot here," Hewitt suggests after a few seconds. Miles nods in response and Mariah glares at him with betrayal and contempt in her eyes. They all know, just like they've always known, Mariah is the best shot with a rifle in her hands. Military training or not, Miles knows he could never compete with her long-range.

"You can't ask me to do this," Mariah whispers. Her eyes have softened from the spiteful look they previously held and in those eyes, it's clear that she knows this is the right thing to do.

"They're going to torture him," Hewitt says. "We can't let that happen. He's dying already and we can definitely make it quick and painless compared to whatever they're planning to do to him over there."

She nods solemnly, agreeing with the truth of what he's saying.

"Let's back up a bit here," Miles begins, skirting back through the lawn to demonstrate that he means the words physically. "There's a house midway down the block that has a perfect window for the shot."

They all know the house he's talking about. They sweep the vacant home as quickly as they can manage before Mariah gets herself installed in the third-floor window, facing the park from just under three blocks away.

"The rain isn't going to make this any easier," she points out.

"Are you able to make the shot from here, or do we need to get somewhere closer?" Miles asks, tension clear in his voice as a silent countdown ticks away the time they're wasting.

"Of course I can," she replies. "The rain lets up here and there, and I've got a clear shot."

Hewitt looks over her shoulder, taking in the scene and nodding in agreement.

"Hewitt," Miles says, "You're with me. We're going to end this shit tonight if we possibly can."

"I'm with you."

"Mariah, give us five minutes to get in place for ourselves. You'll know where we are when the time comes," Miles says, with a grin of determination spreading over his features. "Let's go!"

Hewitt turns to Mariah before leaving the attic, "Brace some shit against that door before you get into position."

Mariah nods and stands up after setting the timer on her phone. She reaches out to Hewitt's cheek and runs her fingers along the familiar contours. "Come back to me, please."

Hewitt silently walks to the door and pulls it shut behind him, wondering if this is the last time he'll see her and refusing to say goodbye because that would be giving voice to that fear. Either one of them, probably both of them, could wind up dead. They are probably all going to be dead before this night is over.

This is all for nothing, Hewitt thinks to himself as he jogs to follow after Miles.

This is one small, secluded community, and Gale had warned them that the same thing was going to be happening globally. It had probably already started. One small town had already cost them so much. Miles stops short and gestures for Hewitt to do the same, distracting him from thoughts he was better dismissing as they were eating away at any last bits of optimism he had left.

"You and I are going to set up a zone here," Miles points to the front doors of two houses at the corner of the block, across the street from each other and directly across the wider lane separating the park from the residential homes.

"We don't have time to clear the houses and dawn isn't far off," he continues, looking around nervously. "Not that it'll make much difference."

"What's the plan?" Hewitt asks.

"I'm sort of making this up as I go, but we're going to set ourselves up with a kill zone right here to pick these fuckers off as they go after Mariah."

"Sounds like a good way to get ourselves fucking murdered, locking ourselves into those houses," Hewitt replies.

"Oh no, my friend, you've got it wrong. We're staying right down here, outside and at the ground level. Our girl is a champ with that rifle back there. You and I are going to be much closer quarters."

Hewitt laughs even though he can feel his testicles crawling up into his abdomen. "You're out of your fucking mind!"

"Maybe," Miles concedes after a moment's thought. "But this is our best shot if we plan to intervene on Abraham's behalf." He gestures to the park.

"I can't argue with you," Hewitt says, still laughing, with what he feels appropriate in calling gallows humor.

"She'll keep on shooting once she's seen our play down here, and we have to trust her to cover us as best she can."

Hewitt glances toward where they'd left Mariah behind. "She will."

"We'll be playing this by ear, pulling back and continuing to fire as we go. We have a lot of room behind us and we'll need to be conscious of our surroundings as we retreat. No rushing. Make every shot count. That shouldn't be a challenge. This is probably going to be what we would call a target-rich environment once it kicks off."

Hewitt takes in the advice and encouragement from his friend, not entirely certain whether he can manage to live up to the expectations Miles is setting. The people up there in the park may not seem to be quite as in charge of their faculties as they had when this had all started off, but there are hundreds of them and only the three of them to hold them off.

Miles looks away, thoughts in line with Hewitt's, his expression distant for a moment. "This is gonna be tense as shit."

"Well, I'd have to say that's an understatement," Hewitt replies.

"Don't worry, my man, I have a few surprises that should help us out. You just stay here behind cover until I start shooting. Stay the fuck out of sight and do not go out in the open until you see me do the same."

Miles winks at Hewitt knowingly, leaving Hewitt to wonder what the hell his friend was talking about. They dart as quickly as they can through the intervening space toward their separate destinations, checking their guns as they run.

43

CHAPTER FORTY-THREE

HEWITT SHIVERS. TUCKED INTO a door frame and willing himself to be smaller and less visible, he is terrified by what comes next. He can't make out where Miles is situated across the street. There's no chance of picking Mariah out in the window of the house further down the street. When the rain lets up a little bit, he can see the house, but she is hidden in her perch.

He's armed, and Miles made sure he's armed well, but he is nervous, more nervous than he's ever been. This whole thing feels like a distorted, nightmarish version of the OK Corral. He's a good shot, and he's quick thinking on his feet, but he has no illusions regarding the fact that he's the weakest link out of the three of them.

In the tense and silent minutes waiting for Mariah to kick things off, Hewitt has plenty of time to analyze his chances and to imagine the worst possible outcomes. He has ample time to internalize the fact that he is about to die and that his death will not be quick or painless.

Miles and Hewitt are out of their minds, waiting down there at street level. Mariah finds herself thinking; knowing what they have planned only makes that assessment more concrete. She had watched them as they ran through the rain and posted themselves down the street and across from one another. It only took her a moment to discern what Miles had in mind and how he and Hewitt would be backing her up. There was no question that they were insane.

She takes her time lining up the shot, with exaggerated care in preparation for something she never imagined she might be doing. This is not what she wants. What she wants is to get the whole disgusting thing over with. What she wants is to wake up in her bed at home and find that this has all been some feverish nightmare. Knowing that the choice has been made for her by circumstances beyond her control, what she wants right now is to never be asked to do anything like this ever again.

Mariah has Abraham in her sights, no question that she will fire true. He looks like he is in agony and she had taken her time in sweeping the crowd before focusing on her dying friend. The jeering, hostile rage painted across the strangers' features is awful and terrifying. As near as she can tell, the disease is progressing just as Gale informed them it would. These people don't have the same predatory glint about them as the mob had just a day before. They're dulling and slowing down. None of this makes the situation better.

She breathes deep a couple of times, calming herself and finding a center, holding the last breath on the exhale and applying slow, steady pressure to the trigger at the same time. The rifle kicks against her shoulder, but she remains steady, sweeping her scope back to verify she has stopped Abraham's suffering. The hole, just off-center on his forehead, is smaller than it seems like it should be, but she knows the exit wound will be substantial. There is no sign of life remaining in their friend.

Hewitt requires a moment to collect himself and realize what's happening when he hears the report from Mariah's shot. He can't see Abraham from where he is, but he can hear the slight shift in the noise of the crowd. Mariah fires three more shots into the crowd before anyone there appears to have any idea what's going on. They don't see her, of course, but they do know the direction the shots are coming from. Two more clean shots and they are moving her way, the mob evenly split between those blindly setting off in her direction and those uncertainly seeking cover.

The latter must be the ones who still have some of their faculties about them, though they still seem to ultimately be swept up in the mob, whether through some herd mentality or simply lacking the wherewithal to fight the tide. Soon enough, the whole cluster of crazed men, women, and children begin to flow like a slow river to where she's still firing.

Mariah focuses on the people most likely to give away her position and those within the group who appear to be moving with the greatest zeal. She will continue firing until she is either out of ammunition or out of luck. Before the first members of the mob have reached the street running along the park, she has taken a total of nine of their number out of the equation. Nine.

Nine more people were dead all because of her friend's madness. Nine more deaths to haunt and torment her for the role she's playing in ending those lives. She buries those thoughts, to be exhumed later, as she relies on instinct and a clear mind to continue firing and reloading quicker than she ever has before.

Hewitt watches as this all takes place, sickened by what they're doing to these poor people and knowing there is no other choice. Hundreds of people press their way through the park and spill into the street while Mariah keeps firing. The teeming mass approaches the road where all three of them are in position.

Heart racing and feeling like his bladder is full and near bursting, Hewitt takes careful aim with his pistol, waiting to be seen or waiting for Miles to signal him that it is time to begin opening fire, uncertain which will come first. Only seconds pass, though it feels like so much longer. The mob is getting closer and the numbers seem overwhelming.

He doesn't see the object landing amid the raging tide, but the loud pop and concussive wave of unexpectedly warm air tell him what Miles meant by surprises. Even with what has to be seventy feet between himself and where the grenade had detonated, he felt it. Hewitt, now knowing what Miles has in mind, flattens himself into his limited cover just before another grenade detonates.

44

CHAPTER FORTY-FOUR

MARIAH HAS NO WAY to respond to what she's just witnessed. She can't even process what she's seen right away. Before she even registers what happened, a second explosion happens and then a third. Shock wears off and she continues firing, angry with herself for having stopped for just those few seconds of impotence. The crowd has noticeably thinned.

From her nest in the window, she can see that there had been probably close to four hundred or maybe even more of the residents spilling out of the park and heading into the residential neighborhood where they'd chosen to take their stand. Only after she's gotten back into her rhythm and fired a few more rounds does she realize that Miles must have had grenades of some kind with him. She would have expected the people to have scattered a bit after the explosions in their midst, but they did not.

"Crazy fucker," she mutters to herself as she takes aim and removes another threat.

Shortly after the third blast, she hears as much as she sees Miles leave cover and begin firing. Three-round bursts, separated by silence, she can tell he is taking careful aim rather than squandering the ammunition. Almost right away, additional gunfire adds its noise to the crescendo as Hewitt fires single rounds from his pistol.

Mariah watches over them, taking her role seriously and selecting her targets more carefully to cover them as they reload and keeping anyone from flanking them and slipping up on either of them from a blind spot.

FEWER THAN HALF OF the initial crowd has gone still. Most of them are still moving in the same direction when Miles begins to fire. He had tried to maximize the effect of each grenade by putting some distance between the separate blasts and focusing on where the crowd was the least dense, hoping to spread the shrapnel to maximum effect. The concussion did a good job of handling the locals immediately surrounding the explosions, but he wasn't satisfied with the results.

He and Hewitt had been too close for comfort, based on his experience, but he'd banked on the crush of bodies being sufficient to keep the two of them safe from the random bits of shrapnel that can, and often do, travel well outside of the standard blast radius. It looks like he was right since Hewitt joins him in firing on the front wave of attackers.

He wishes he'd had more than just the three M67s and would have gladly settled for even a MK3A2 or two as well. The reality is that he only ever had the three grenades as a joke more than anything else. His friends teased him for being a firearm aficionado, all in good fun, and he'd procured the fragmentation grenades mostly to take their joke and run with it. He'd show them a gun nut if that's what they wanted to see.

The present circumstances make him wish he'd really been as paranoid and over the top as his friends characterized him as being. A couple more grenades, even just some concussion cylinders, would make simpler work of the remaining locals.

As it stands, he figures he managed to kill, or at least cripple, somewhere near a hundred of the enemy with the three grenades he'd used. The same density of the crowd that sheltered him and Hewitt from shrapnel also cut down on the effectiveness of each blast. There are a lot more injured than dead, but anyone not crippled by their injuries is still coming as if nothing had happened, just angrier and more insane if such a thing is even possible. They aren't coming fast though, and that is the only relief he sees in the situation.

The MP5 had always been one of his favorite guns and she was working like a dream for him right now. Conserving ammunition, he continues with three-round bursts, target after target, while he and Hewitt converge at the center of the lane and begin slowly backing their way down the block and toward the impossible distance they'll need to cover to get back to Mariah. Miles had expected they would be running for cover, but rapidly backing along is enough of a chore that it begins wearing them both down.

They can still hear their guardian angel firing and both men find comfort in knowing that she's covering them and watching their backs. Hewitt ejects the final magazine from his handgun and swings the Mossberg 500 12-gauge off his shoulder.

As primed as he is, he's almost too slow. A man from the crowd lunges at him, howling unintelligibly. The barrel of

Hewitt's shotgun is shoved downward as the man closes in, but he squeezes the trigger just the same and the attacker is hit where his right hip meets his abdomen. The man stays upright for only a moment until his weight shifts to his useless right leg and he finally collapses.

Hewitt continues firing. Other members of the crowd had closed in on him during the brief engagement. Eight rounds, then reload. He saves his shots for when they count the most, knowing that range is not his friend with this one. The two men slip into a routine where Hewitt focuses on closer targets while Miles tackles the ones further away.

Ears are ringing with the telltale signs of damage that will surely lead to tinnitus. Ear protection wasn't really an option for them and hadn't been a priority to procure, but they're alive so far, and that's better than the alternative. The semi-organized retreat to where Mariah is holed up seems to stretch on forever, but the two of them back through the gate and down the sidewalk to the porch only a matter of minutes after the first grenade's detonation.

The narrow entrance to the yard itself provided by the sturdy gate and wrought-iron fence allows Miles and Hewitt to take their time a little bit more and to block the path with bodies, slowing the fifty or so locals still approaching. Some of the more determined try to climb the fence, but they're easy enough for Mariah to pick off from above. There seems to be no real cunning left in these people, just a pure hate-fueled drive to keep on pushing forward, to reach the three of them and kill. Hewitt wonders if these people are so far gone that they'll be eaten as well and whether they will still be alive when it happens.

Ammunition is running low, but so are the numbers of infected still on the offensive. The same logistics apply as on the street, bodies on the ground slow the ones still coming, but they are steadily closing the gap faster than Miles and Hewitt can plug it. The plan had never been to retreat into the house, but then again, Hewitt wonders if the plan ever really accounted for them surviving this long against these odds.

Backed against the wall and the door respectively, the two men face down the final dozen locals still pressing forward, more like the zombies at this point than the riled-up mob they'd appeared to be in the park. Miles finally understands why the grenades hadn't scattered them at all, seeing what had been clear to Mariah for a while. These people are all right on the verge of letting go of those last little remnants of humanity inside of them. Hewitt sees it too, though he's been noticing the same thing for a short while.

Hewitt begins to suspect that the planned execution of Abraham might have been the final volitional act for all of these people. Even then, he believes they were on autopilot more than actually making any sort of actual choice. It is with sadness and sympathy that Hewitt fires the final round from the shotgun, dropping a young woman, barely clothed, who had made it onto the porch to his left. Reversing his grip, he bashes the stock into the temple of a boy behind her.

Miles is down to only a few rounds in his 9mm and he's trying to make them count. Those final rounds don't last long. They have nowhere further to fall back to, backs pressed against the wall, the final members of the mob closing in more quickly than either of them would like.

The door opens behind Miles and he almost falls backward into Mariah as she steps through the opening and begins firing from her handgun, having left the rifle upstairs since range no longer mattered. Hewitt and Miles are both painfully aware of the fact that Mariah has saved their asses at the last possible moment. There is no relief to be felt by any of them as the final approaching member of the crowd falls heavily to the ground, no longer animated and no longer a threat.

There is only crushing exhaustion and dismay. Now, as the adrenaline fades, they register what they've done. A crushing weight presses down on all of their heads. Abraham was dead. They were returning to the mine without Ben's dad, and that might have been the only parent the boy had left.

45

— · —

Chapter Forty-Five

After almost a solid week of overcast skies and rain, the sun breaking through the clouds seems like it should be met with more enthusiasm than an exhaled and bone-weary Hewitt can manage to pull off. *How long has it been?* He wonders to himself. *Has it really been only a few days since the rain began?*

His back pressed against the rough wall of stone just outside the mine entrance, only a couple of feet from where Gale had taken his life, Hewitt starts to lose circulation in his legs from the way he has them folded beneath him. He shifts restlessly against the numbness and tingling until the pins and needles begin to fade.

The conversation with Ben had gone about as well as he could have expected. Better than he worried it might go, actually. Much of the calm response on Ben's part could have come from shock, but Hewitt's pretty sure he's just got a lot of his dad in him. Sure, the boy had cried, and Mariah had wrapped her arms around him and silently let the boy grieve. But he'd remained calm despite the obviously excruciating pain. After he'd worn himself out from crying, he fell almost immediately asleep.

Hewitt remained awake long enough to see everyone else asleep, and the sleep he did receive was fitful at best.

If he was having nightmares, he couldn't remember any of them. He didn't need nightmares, though. His reality has become scary enough. He finally gives up on trying.

No one else is awake and he can't seem to make himself sleep any more than he already has. Every time he closes his eyes he sees the same horrible things he's been participating in since this nightmare all began. Each time he begins to fall asleep, he sees himself surrounded by ravenous monsters with the familiar faces of friends and long lost loved ones. There was no comfort or peace to be found in slumber when even sleep was no respite from the nightmares.

From the angle he's seated he can't see the town past the pines towering all around and that is as close to rest as he's going to get, especially now that the clouds are beginning to break up, allowing the sun to send some glorious illumination down toward the mountain across the valley from where he sits. For just a moment or two, he can almost forget the things he's had to do and the things still ahead of him, and he can breathe in the pristine and untouched beauty that captivated him during their first days here.

Miles, he thinks, may have the stomach for this sort of thing, but he truly doubts that he has much left in the tank. Days of carnage, trauma, and a perpetual state of terror have eroded any sense he had of being clean or human, and he sincerely suspects the others feel the same. He hopes there's that much left of who they once were, that this experience hasn't consumed everything good or optimistic, like it threatens to do to him.

Still sitting in the same place, he doesn't hear the scuffing of footsteps approaching him from behind and he jumps when Miles speaks, "It's still quite beautiful up here."

"Until you know, you remember the violence, the blood on our hands and soaking into the soil down there," he replies, his voice hollow and lacking any real inflection. "And, of course, everything we've lost."

"There is that," Miles replies quickly, "and we had all better remember that, and never forget it."

Hewitt looks up at his friend, his expression making the confusion he feels plain to Miles.

"This shit," he answers the unspoken question. "The things we've been forced to do. You may want to forget it. It's only natural to want exactly that, but I hope you never do. You need to remember everything about it, including how dirty and low it made you feel. You're dishonoring these people, the strangers, and our friends if you allow yourself to forget them. Enemies, especially enemies who had no choice; they deserve our respect and remembrance."

"That is some strange fucking advice, my friend," Hewitt says.

Miles shrugs. "Maybe strange, but it's true. If you allow yourself to forget these people, you're taking your first steps toward being a bigger monster than what we've seen out there. That's how you become the sort of person who can just do this kind of thing and walk away content."

Hewitt has no response. He silently mulls over what his friend has said, thinking about all the strangers he'd hurt or killed since all of this started. He's lost in thought, not taking in anything in front of him anymore, and he doesn't notice when Miles returns to the mine interior and the lab beyond. When he finally returns from his internal musings, he realizes that he's alone again.

Gazing off into the distance, Hewitt shifts his thinking from the atrocities already committed to those he knows are still to come. Down there, lurking in the remaining shadows, are dozens or even hundreds of people, or what used to be people. They may not still be quite accurately described as people, but Miles' words force him to remember that these were men, women, and children who had lives before all of this. They had dreams, pasts, and futures until Gale turned everything topsy-turvy.

This isn't over for any of them, the nightmare continues, though for the folks down the hill he sincerely hopes that any part of them that might have been human has left the building long before now. That's the least they deserve.

46

Chapter Forty-Six

COMPARING THE POPULATION STATISTICS with the dead they'd discovered on their attempt to sweep and clear the town as well as those they'd dispatched for themselves, only about a quarter of the locals are unaccounted for and could still be out there. The numbers are daunting, but when compared to what they'd already dealt with, it is something manageable even with just the three of them on the hunt. Ben, whether he likes it or not, is not participating in this final act of defiance against the world Gale ushered in.

As confident as they try to be, each of them has their suspicions that what's coming is going to be a suicide mission. It is going to be rough, it would have been even if all six of them were still around, but left to just them, it is going to be virtually impossible.

If Gale's projections remain accurate, and so far they've been horrifying in their accuracy and precision, it should only be the zombie-like individuals out there now, shambling around and consuming whatever they can find. There may be some exceptions, Gale had even suggested that genetic variance could allow for natural immunity or at least immune responses that would dramatically slow the process, but most of what they know they'll be seeing is the later stage infected, shuffling their way to certain death.

The sun had started shining again at just the right time. Darkness isn't their ally anymore, they all agree. What they're gearing up to fight now isn't an enemy who will exhibit any guile or strategy. Even the most recent encounter with the higher functioning residents had been largely bereft of any sort of cunning. Once they have the attention of the things out there, they should all start coming out of the woodwork.

The plan seems solid as they've worked it out, albeit insane, but there are too many unknowns for any of them to feel good about their chances. They begin by checking homes and businesses they'd already cleared, making certain nothing has changed concerning those properties that fall along their path between the mine and the location they've picked for the final offensive. Miles is very clear that they don't want their rear any more exposed than it has to be while they are getting into position, and neither Mariah nor Hewitt have any objections.

All but two of the locations had remained clear and, rather than feel the time is wasted, Hewitt took the opportunity to begin taking a rough inventory of anything worth noting in each home. Mariah and Miles begin doing the same. Progress is slow, especially with the rough inventory taking place, but aided by the daylight, it goes more quickly than when they'd previously visited each of the homes in the middle of the night. It's surreal returning to some of these places in the light of day.

Resistance is less than what they expected and certainly less than what they'd experienced before. Only five of the zombified residents await them as they make their way through the center of town and to the neighborhood surrounding the park. Still attempting to maintain some operational silence as well as they can hope to keep from announcing their presence for a while still, they avoid using any of the firearms they're carrying, also hoping to conserve ammunition until they need it.

As they come closer to the park and the site of the massacre from only a couple of nights before, they all begin to gag on the foul odor of rot and excrement that forms a miasma all around them. They knew it would be bad, but seeing the dead littering the ground and breathing it in during the midday sun paints it all in such a vividly gruesome detail that even Miles has to fight the urge to vomit in anticipation of what they're approaching, knowing it will be worse before it gets better.

Sure enough, the sights and smells only get worse as they get closer to the park. The site of numerous executions has become a buffet for some of the ravenous and nearly dead. The sounds of snarls and of flesh being ripped away and consumed warn them of what's coming before they get within sight of the park itself. Wary, and with guns drawn, the trio approaches the area as cautiously as they've ever done anything in their lives.

Through the carnage stretching out before them, a dozen of the townsfolk crawl amidst the bodies of the dead, eating everything they can tear away with either fingers or teeth, the nearly dead gorging themselves on those who beat them to the finish line. None of them take notice of the friends as they approach the gruesome outdoor abattoir. In the disorienting flurry of a couple of nights before, in the shadows lit only by muzzle flashes and lighting, none of them had been able to take in the extent of the slaughter.

Hewitt feels dizzy while looking around, knowing he is personally responsible for so much of this death and not knowing how to process that knowledge in a way that makes sense. "Holy shit," he mutters under his breath, the only words any of them can bring themselves to speak. The awful soundtrack of the feast taking place around them accompanies a vision that is no less terrible.

With exaggerated care, they make their way through the bodies strewn across the ground, keeping as much distance between themselves and the infected as they can pull off without altering their course too much. Directly ahead of them looms the small non-denominational chapel, seemingly ominous in its apparent peaceful tranquility while the battlefield surrounds them. The chapel itself isn't what fills Hewitt and his friends with dread, so much as what the place is meant to become once they get there.

This will be the location of their last stand in this dead town, the final battle before they either fall from the weight of unnatural monsters or they prepare themselves for a return to an outside world that may already be collapsing beneath the pressure brought about by Gale's plague. None of them know whether they will survive this final stroke in their plan. In the next minutes or hours, it could be only Ben who remains alive and well to leave this awful place.

Beyond the sights, sounds, and smells of the journey through the town itself and into the park, their final stretch to reach the chapel is safe and uneventful, the zombies behind them too preoccupied with their meal to notice the living who have slipped through the area like the ghosts Hewitt suspects they will all soon become.

The door is unlocked and Miles bursts through the door first, sweeping a Mossberg shotgun through the open space. The place smells clean, but they can't afford to take any chances; so Miles treats the open plan of the church like any other building they'd entered on the way here.The place turns out to be an empty sanctuary. For the time being, the chapel is the safe and peaceful place its builders intended it to be.

None of the three of them consider themselves particularly spiritual or religious individuals, but both Miles and Mariah silently whisper their own sort of prayers, whether to some potential deity or to the universe itself, hoping that something might be listening but knowing that they're all alone in this. Hewitt silently reflects on the fact that this will more than likely be his last day on Earth, and he finds himself struggling to make peace with that fact. As many times as he's passively waited for death to find him or entertained the thought of going out looking for himself, he's not ready and he certainly doesn't want his friends dragged down with him.

The chapel bell has been updated to an electronic control but, as Hewitt hoped when concocting this plan, there is a manual control for the armature that gets the bell swinging so the clapper can do its job.

"Do you really think this will work, buddy?" Miles asks, looking over the bell controls.

"It's the best suggestion I've got," Hewitt shrugs. "There's no reason this shouldn't work, and if we don't get them all in one place, it's pretty fucking unlikely we'll ever get them all."

"Seems risky, you know, drawing a hundred or more of those things to us here."

"No more risk, I figure, than trying to hunt them down house by house, room by room. At least, assuming this works, we'll have an open space to work with, none of that bullshit with them sneaking up behind us and no hidden corners to account for."

Miles shrugs.

"Target-rich environment, right?" Hewitt grins sadly.

"That's for damn sure," Miles says.

"It's a good plan, baby," Mariah says, walking up from behind him and taking Hewitt's hand. She squeezes tightly, tighter than Hewitt thinks she realizes. He can tell from the pressure that she's just as scared as he is. Miles may mask it better, but he suspects they're all about equally terrified with what they're about to do.

The three stand there in silence for a few minutes, taking in the illusory tranquility and peacefulness, no remnant inside of this place of the horrors they've experienced, nothing intruding on the space they're in; nothing but the emotional scars and haunted recollections they've carried in with them.

Hewitt cranks the arm and gets the bell ringing. Inside the building, it is a jarring onslaught of noise, even for ears that will probably be experiencing permanent ringing from being unprotected in the presence of so much gunfire only a couple of nights before.

Even through the din inside, they can hear the bell's clanging resounding through town and echoing back from buildings and the valley walls surrounding the place. Hewitt swears he can hear the groans and hungry moaning of the damned revenants rising to add their own dissonant chorus to the awful tune sweeping through the dead place that once was their home. It's a haunting sound that none of them will ever forget, whether they live long lives or, more likely, they reach the end of their respective journeys today.

AT THE MOUTH OF the mine, staring out over the handful of rooftops that appear through the dense tree growth, Ben hears the bell and the moaning that picks up to accompany it. The sounds carried to him on a breeze that chills him far less than the tuneless song itself.

For the first time since watching the others depart, Ben worries that his father's friends will not be returning. He'll be trapped here alone with however many of the monsters are left. He imagines hundreds of the prematurely decaying revenants crawling and stumbling their way to the mine, the black pits of their gaping mouths a shared conduit to an abyss from which he'll never escape. And leading the shuffling mass is his father, guiding the hungry horde to feast on him, as much as a mindless slave to that hunger as the rest.

He knows they aren't actually zombies, and he knows his father isn't going to rise from the dead to torment him, but that doesn't stop the terrible visions from plaguing his thoughts, unbidden. Ben feels listless. He wishes he could be down there with the other three. He should be helping them. Maybe one more person is all the difference between survival and death—for all of them. A dozen times or more, those intrusive thoughts have pushed him to leave the lab and make his way into the center of town.

It wasn't that he was listening to the others, that he remained sealed up in safety, though. He was afraid. He was so afraid. And he was alone. He'd pushed through the fear before, but it was paralyzing him now. How could he tell his mom about what happened?

Was she even still alive for him to tell her anything at all? Was anyone he knew still alive? Was there even still a world out there beyond the flooded valley at the edge of town?

47

CHAPTER FORTY-SEVEN

"HOLY SHIT," HEWITT WHISPERS in awe, terror causing every muscle to tense up in mortification. "If only Romero was still around to witness this. It's like that opening scene from Day of the Dead."

Miles chuckles, having had similar thoughts of his own over the last few days.

"Yeah, but we sadly do not have a chopper to fly us away to safety," Mariah points out, concerned that the men aren't taking the situation seriously enough.

"Assuming anywhere is safe after this," Hewitt remarks, giving voice to fears he hasn't been able to shake since Gale had shared his plans with them. His fear is that the rest of the world will be no different when, or if, they ever leave this place.

New voices keep adding their own off-key baritone to the awful dirge outside, and though he knows better, it sounds to Hewitt as if there are more of the zombies heading their way than there had been people in the mob a couple of days before. He knows he's wrong. He did the math himself and the math added up. The dead aren't rising from their graves, these aren't actually zombies. There can't be more than one hundred and fifty to two hundred people left moving in town.

He has to keep reminding himself that they are ready for this and that they've been through worse already; though the profound smell that continues making him want to gag has him feeling like he's been lying to himself.

"They're slow but unrelenting," Miles offers as encouragement and warning all in one. "On the positive side, we don't need to aim exclusively for the head like they do in the movies. Center mass does the trick just as well."

The sound from outside continues growing louder as the remaining residents swarm toward the source of the noise that may as well have been a dinner bell.

"Center mass gives you a shot at heart, lungs, or even the spine and if you hit any of those, it should knock any of these shambling fucks out of commission," Miles says before glancing at Hewitt. "Target-rich environment!"

"One hell of a pep talk there, Miles," Mariah says. "Practice that one in front of the mirror this morning?"

"Why yes, my dear, I did. How kind of you to notice? I stood naked before the mirror, beholding myself as I went through the whole speech, and then I jerked off into the eggs we had for breakfast."

Hewitt barely stifles a snort, and just like that, the tension in the air is lifted and the weight of what's coming suddenly feels less unbearable and beyond their abilities. He's not confident about the odds, but he's not ready to give up either.

"Fuck you both," Mariah says. Her tone is stern, but a glance over his shoulder and Hewitt is rewarded with a shit-eating grin. The three of them begin laughing, and for just a moment it drowns out the noise growing in intensity outside. For Mariah, it feels like a symbolic victory, the sort of symbol she focused on in her teaching. This moment is representative of their little band of misfits being greater than the throngs of monsters ushered their way by the base, animal desire to kill and to devour.

"I suppose it's time to go," Hewitt says, slipping earplugs into place and feeling like he might just be wasting his time with the precaution, judging by the constant ringing in his ears since the other night. The others do the same and similarly wonder if they're maybe just a bit late to the party in considering ear protection.

Miles is the first through the door, seeing two dozen of the nearly dead residents crossing the church lawn from the park, and there are so many more behind them. Taking a weaver stance, he begins firing at those at the center. Hewitt and Mariah follow him through and take up positions to the right and left of Miles, focusing their fire on their respective sides of the field. The plan in this, as Miles explained it, is to minimize any risk of wasting rounds on anyone else's target.

Miles and Mariah begin by making a good show of it, mostly managing single-shot kills. Hewitt takes a little longer getting a handle on things, wasting two or even three rounds on the first few targets, emptying the magazine without much to show for it. The next magazine goes much further, and the bodies begin piling up in his kill zone as well. The earplugs aren't much help, but he recalls how much worse it had been the other night, and he's grateful for anything that might take the edge off.

Miles can't help but wish the odor of primer would be a little more potent, the acrid scent of gunfire being largely lost outdoors, anything would be better than the smell of sickness and human waste that barely masks the rot hanging in the air already. In fiction, there's always that overpowering scent that accompanies a discharged firearm and he has never, in all his years before now, wished more for that to be true. Sadly, nothing is ever likely to wash away this awful smell, and certainly, nothing will scrub his mind of the memory of it.

They just keep coming, crawling over the rising obstruction formed by the truly dead. In a semi-circle around them lay dozens of dead, haphazardly stacked and scattered as they've fallen or been shoved aside by their oncoming comrades. Stumbling and slipping their way forward, the newcomers show no fear or awareness of those who came before them.

Miles' handgun jams, and rather than bother with clearing the action, he grabs another, switching them out in the holster. He's impressed that this is the first, considering they've fired more than a hundred rounds between them. His guns were always well-maintained, but with circumstances like this, he almost expected luck to be working against them.

There is no marking the passage of time, but the longer the onslaught lasts, the more they can take their time. The zombies aren't graceful or dexterous and the obstacle course of corpses provides some respite as arms and shoulders begin to feel numb, especially after the strenuous night they only just recovered from. Even as lightweight as the guns happen to be, the strength to keep firing with any accuracy is limited.

Finally, though, the wretched groaning of the horde is done as the final echoes of gunfire bounce through the town.

"So," Mariah begins, "Which of you big, strong men is cleaning this shit up?" She slumps exhausted to the ground and the others follow her lead.

"I say we make the kid do it," Miles says, laughing until the dryness of his throat turns the laughter to a coughing fit.

"I'm sure his dad made him do chores, right?" Hewitt adds. None of them have the energy left to laugh, but they all sit there smiling until the smell finally forces them to move.

BEN THROWS HIS ARMS around Hewitt as the three return to the lab, smelling awful and somehow looking worse. Hewitt returns the embrace, having been just as uncertain that they'd see each other again as Ben had been when he heard the bells followed by the reports of gunfire. Miles pats the boy on the shoulder as he passes.

"I'm taking a long fucking shower in the hottest water possible. I might just go through decontamination while I'm at it."

Mariah closes the door to the lab and walks to where Ben and Hewitt are still hugging, putting her arms around both of them. The three of them had discussed it on their way back up the hill, and Hewitt had been nominated as the one to talk things over with Ben. He is the one most bonded with the boy. Mariah insinuated this was due to Hewitt being a child himself, even though he was approaching forty.

"Ben," Hewitt begins as soon as he and the young man had parted from their embrace, "we've got a lot of work to do down there, as I expect you know."

The boy only nods in response, still feeling overcome by his relief at knowing he wasn't going to be alone.

"Taking inventory of supplies and resources in town is going to be a long project and we will need your help." He pauses, trying to find a gentler way to tackle the next part and deciding that he's better off just powering through. "You worked with your old man a lot, on job sites and whatnot. Right?"

"Yes I did," Ben replies proudly.

"That's good! Have you ever handled heavy equipment at all?"

The boy affirms that he has and proceeds to go into detail, telling Hewitt and Mariah about driving front-loaders, backhoes, and even handling a crane once. Hewitt wants to cry, hearing so much of Abraham in his son's voice and the way he talks about these things. Mariah shares similar sentiments as she turns away and tries to wipe at her eyes inconspicuously.

"Would you be able to teach me how to use the equipment here in town?" Hewitt finally asks, getting to the big question. In response to the boy's quizzical look, Hewitt explains that they need to dispose of the bodies somehow, and as much as they have tried to think of an alternate solution because they want to be respectful, they have no choice but to be practical about it.

He takes his time telling Ben that they want to bury his father, Kateb, Deputy Weber, and even Gale the right way, but that doing the same sort of thing for the more than a thousand people who lived here in town, just simply isn't possible.

"It's going to sound terrible," he continues, "but we want to dig a mass grave at the edge of the existing cemetery near the chapel. We're going to burn the bodies in the grave to keep scavengers from finding them and to keep other diseases from popping up. To do this, I need you to teach me how to use the tractors and heavy equipment I'm going to be operating."

"I can do it," Ben says without hesitation, taking both Hewitt and Mariah by surprise. "It's what my dad would do if he was still here with us. It's what he would want me to do, too."

"I don't think your dad would want anything like that," Mariah says, stunned by the boy's mature response. Ben looks at her and cracks an altogether too familiar smile.

"Dad always worked hard, and he expected it from everyone else around him. If there was a job to be done and someone who could do it but didn't, it would disappoint him, even if he didn't say it. He didn't have any use for people who disappointed him."

Hewitt can't resist but to crack a smile, knowing at that moment how much his friend still lived on through the young man in front of him. There was no question as to just how proud Abraham would be.

"You're right about that," Hewitt acknowledges. "Your old man pushed me to work harder on plenty of occasions."

Hewitt pauses, thinking things over for a minute, weighing the options before continuing. "You are welcome to help, but this is not going to be fun work and if you lose the stomach for it, we all understand and no one will blame you. I still need you to teach me though, because you aren't going to be doing this work alone."

Ben agrees, and they shake on it with an exaggerated caricature of making a deal. A shower is in order for Hewitt and Mariah, and they choose to do so together after Miles is finished. Neither of them feels any urge for intimacy beyond simply being close and holding each other tightly, thankful that they've managed to survive all of this together, against all odds.

They stand there for ten minutes, beneath a steady stream of nearly scalding water that they wish could somehow make them feel clean after everything, holding onto one another as if each is afraid the other might float away if they let go. Finally, they wash one another with tenderness and care before drying off and retreating to the room they've been sharing, skin wrinkled from the water.

48

CHAPTER FORTY-EIGHT

Everyone sleeps through the night for the first time since the fateful evening of Kateb's death and there is no rush to get moving the following morning. Once they've all gotten up and moving, they fall into an unspoken routine, knowing the first thing they need to do.

The early afternoon finds them, sweating and covered in dirt and mud, standing before four fresh graves with crude markers displaying only the names of their fallen friends and nothing more. There are no words to say over the resting places and there have hardly been any words spoken between the four of them since waking. With the same unspoken connection, they turn away from the graves and prepare to get started on the work that can't be put off any longer.

While Ben helps Hewitt maneuver heavy equipment from the Emergency Services Building, Miles and Mariah begin to load bodies onto a flatbed trailer, thankful that the lab was fully equipped with HazMat suits so that they could dress appropriately for the occasion.

It's an exhausting and emotionally taxing day, but they make progress and with Miles' systematic approach, he and Mariah manage to remove the dead from close to half of the town, only encountering one remaining zombie, trapped in a fenced yard and dragging a useless broken leg behind it as it digs claws into the earth to move itself toward them.

The hole for the grave completed, Hewitt and Ben join the other two the following morning for more of the same cleanup, from dawn until dusk. The more they clear out the dead, the more they find themselves alone in what is feeling more and more like a ghost town.

DAY THREE OF THE cleanup is the hardest for Hewitt by far. Having to do something he has been dreading since the talk of a mass grave had first come up, he feels unclean. Using the diesel-powered front-loader, he scoops bodies from the festering, insect-ridden piles and drops them into the pit already filling with the bodies they'd hauled in by trailer.

When it concerned the remnants of the final defense, they all knew it wouldn't make sense to transport the dead, body by body. This is the gruesome chore he'd had in mind when he asked Ben to walk him through operating this beast, and this is a chore he left for himself as penance for the guilt he knows he shouldn't be feeling. The work is worse than he imagined it could be, but it needs to be done.

As he lifts and deposits the dead into their final resting place, the other three go home to home, collecting what they need and making note of anything they aren't loading into the bed of the massive Chevy truck Miles picked out for the task. While their work is time-consuming and certainly exhausting in its way, none of them would trade their labor for what Hewitt is doing.

Evening comes and the other three join Hewitt at the park where he's finished dousing the pit and its contents with gasoline and kerosene since he had both in ready supply and he wants to get this over with quickly and doesn't want to take any chances with the final stage of the job. Standing together, at what they hope is a safe distance from the grave, Hewitt hands Miles one of the road flares while keeping the other for himself. "You want to share this dubious honor with me?" He asks.

Miles nods solemnly and the two ignite the flares in unison. They toss the flares to opposite sides of the hole and at first nothing happens, leaving Hewitt feeling like he'd fucked something up somehow. With a powerful whoosh, the vapor ignites, sending a burst of flame into the sky in a massive ball that rocks them all back on their heels.

They watch the fire burning, trying to stay upwind of the smoke until the stars appear above them in the sky. The fire still burning, but safely contained in the grave, the four of them climb into the truck and return to the mine. The haze of smoke from the still burning pit turns their stomachs the following morning and they complete their inventory with masks over their faces. Hewitt and Miles spend a while trying to decide which smell is worse, the victims before the grave or after the fire and neither of them can decide.

Before twilight, Hewitt and Ben drop loads of dirt over the still smoldering bodies, covering the remnants of the massacre and leaving the tamped down soil as a new hill at the edge of the cemetery grounds.

49

— . —

Chapter Forty-Nine

Once the fighting is finally over, it becomes a sort of relief that they are in a small town nestled into the Northwestern Rocky Mountains. Miles may have carried an arsenal of sorts with him wherever he went, but there are more guns in the town than they could conceivably use. Thankfully, there is a complimentary surplus of ammunition, along with several reloaders in various sheds and garages throughout the town.

All told, they collect more than a hundred separate firearms, a dozen or so compound bows, and a plethora of knives ranging from the tactical to the ludicrous fantasy blades of teenagers altogether too obsessed with fantasy worlds. Miles wouldn't be able to load a fraction of the surplus into his SUV, so he begins sorting through the supplies to set aside the best maintained and most useful. As efficient as he is, Hewitt can see how disappointed Miles is whenever something is set aside in the pile of excess they won't be carrying with them.

It almost makes him smile. How silly it is that Miles loves these guns so much, and so openly. One thing is certain, they are starting the apocalypse on the right sort of footing, with a militia's worth of armaments at their fingertips. Life in the mountains could be rough, and many of the homes had food and water stores that could potentially last for years. The four of them had their pick when it came to things like MREs, canned goods, and dehydrated or otherwise preserved items.

It seemed like the whole population had been prepared for long, harsh winters, or there was an exceedingly large proportion of doomsday preppers in the region. Hewitt wouldn't have been surprised if it was an even split, but either way, they could benefit from the preparations of the former residents.

A quick inventory puts them at more than a year's worth of supplies without any severe rationing involved, as long as it remains just the four of them. In dire straits, they could probably manage to stretch out what they have for nearer three years, and they haven't scavenged every residence yet.

Miles' SUV is going to be the best available option for getting out of town and back to the real world. Combining the space and fuel economy, they weren't finding anything else in town that would compare favorably, not that would pull the small trailer they planned to haul with them, at least. Based on the projections Gale had shared with them, they couldn't count on being able to safely resupply once they are on the road.

Between the cleanup and the scavenging, they had spent another exhausting week in this god-forsaken town. Hewitt hadn't been sleeping much, not beyond the little bit of sleep he involuntarily received when he had nodded off in Gale's laboratory while studying the tests and documentation Gale had left behind.

Mariah had taken to sleeping in there as well, just to be close to him and to make sure he didn't need anything. Mostly she stuck around to be sure that he hadn't been getting too wrapped up in Gale's insanity or just as wrapped up in his own head.

Ben and Miles had become inseparable during the days following Abraham's death. For his part, Miles was acting in a capacity somewhere between father-figure and big brother, and it seemed to be working. Having never even considered being a father himself, Miles seems to be a natural. In some sense, he was filling the void left by Kateb's passing, but he was ultimately just doing what he felt was right in honoring Abraham's memory. For Miles, it was a matter of doing the decent thing.

Ben is coping with everything, from the violence and terror to the loss of his father, with more poise than any of them could have expected from a child his age. He is his father's son.

For all the necessary preparations they make and the work they have yet to do, they all feel like they are spinning their wheels and wasting time that they don't know they have. None of them is willing to rush blindly and unprepared into the world beyond this mountain valley, but they feel quite acutely that they are losing valuable time. It was a fantasy. They all know it, ever believing they could get ahead of this thing, but it is a fantasy they still cling tightly to.

50

—·—

Chapter Fifty

The smell of burning bodies from the mass grave is something Hewitt doesn't believe he will ever forget. There was no other practical solution for disposing of the thousand plus corpses in anything approaching a timely manner and especially when attempting to avoid a swarm of vermin and insects being drawn to the town as temperatures rise with the approach of summer. He feels like he is in a concentration camp or Bosnia, participating in something so grotesque and terrible. It is no consolation that he had no choice.

The only bodies not added to the pyre were Kateb, Abraham, Gale, and the deputy. Even Miles, as angry and betrayed as he felt, couldn't bring himself to toss Gale into the pile. There was no doubt in any of their minds that it was precisely what he deserved, but he had still been their friend for almost their whole lives and none of them could be so cold.

Gale's actions had made them all complicit in monstrous actions, necessary ones, but no less horrifying for there having been no other choice. They had all seen war now, the worst parts of it, as Miles had informed them, unsolicited.

In all his years of military service and subsequent private contracting, he'd never experienced anything quite this terrible. Men, women, and children, all of them American citizens, each and every one. These people hadn't been enemy combatants or terrorists. They were just sick people who had no more control over how they were behaving than a rabid animal would. And, just like rabid animals, there was no way to cure or save them. The sickness had gone too far.

Gale had made it clear that there was no way to halt or reverse the damage done to the infected once it was in their systems. He may have been a mass-murdering asshole when it all came down to it, but he wouldn't have lied about that. Gale had spent some time attempting to work out a vaccine of sorts, something preventative, but it was work he'd needed to perform all by himself since no one within the CDC would have approved of the nightmarish pet project he'd undertaken of his own initiative under their noses. He had made some progress, but not nearly enough, and now he was gone.

"War makes monsters of us all," Miles mutters to himself, echoing the similar thoughts in Hewitt's mind.

"How much worse is it going to be out there?" Mariah asks, gesturing in the general direction of the valley entrance. Hewitt shakes his head in silence, and moments later, Miles does the same.

"No point in asking that question," Miles replies. "We can try to prepare ourselves for what's going on out there, but there ain't any preparing for shit like this."

"You've got that right," Hewitt says as he slumps to the ground with his back against the wall of the barn. From where she's standing, Mariah can finally see the tears in Hewitt's eyes.

"This is a fucking nightmare," Mariah whispers to herself, her voice lost in the sound of the flames nearby. Ash is picked up and deposited by the wind, coating each of them no matter how hard they attempt to remind up-wind of the fire.

It's near impossible to feel clean with the ash from thousands of burning corpses clinging to your skin and hair, finding its way into your nostrils and mouth and clinging there, staining your face where tears attempt to clean the skin. As acclimated to horror as Miles has become over the years, he knows that he will never feel clean again, just like his friends.

51

— · —

CHAPTER FIFTY-ONE

WE'RE TOO LATE, THEY all think simultaneously, the realization hitting each of them like a physical blow. Miles slams his foot down on the brakes, unable to concentrate on the road ahead of him. The voice of the radio host is professional, but there is more than a hint of barely contained panic beneath the tranquil surface, eroding that veneer of professional detachment just slightly.

It was happening everywhere. They'd only just been able to receive something other than static on the radio, and they all wished they could've had a few more minutes of white noise, now that they were hearing something else.

Gale's project was as successful as he predicted it would be; as much as they'd all hoped it was hubris and that Gale had missed something, they had all known, somewhere deep down inside, that their friend would have considered everything before implementing something of this scale. Gale had been nothing if not meticulous.

If Hewitt were to review the computer logs back in the lab, he suspects he would find records of dozens of models run with projections that shored up Gale's confidence. He'd never been the type to overlook even the tiniest detail, their friend's intellect proportional to his apparent lack of empathy or humanity.

The knowledge that society, as they knew it, was collapsing on a global scale weighs heavily on Hewitt's shoulders, even though he knows he wasn't the cause of this. Regardless of how adamant Gale had been that this was his way to save Hewitt from a fate like Tristan's, he knows that he played no part in bringing this tragedy about. Internalizing what he knows to be true intellectually has been proving to be more challenging.

Nothing quite washes away the guilt he feels. Perhaps nothing ever will. What had transpired in this formerly quaint little town had been merely a microcosm, a test run to put his friends through a gauntlet. The rest of the world is now experiencing what Gale's trial run had subjected them to, and it is not going well out there.

It seems to be spreading so fast out there in the real world, and the standard ingrained responses to epidemic or pandemic conditions are only accelerating the spread. Attempting to quarantine the sick and requesting the public contact the authorities regarding anyone they believe to be ill is only serving to fuel the paranoia and in/out-group distrust by persons symptomatic of the first stages of illness.

Similarly, quarantine only serves to cluster together large groups of the infected, which inevitably makes them more difficult to manage once they turn and become ravenous beasts.

Listening to the reports being broadcast, they know it is going to take altogether too long before people begin reacting in the only way that will put an end to this plague, putting down the infected before they transform into the inhuman threat they would ultimately become. There will be no treatment and no cure for this, but the authorities are going to let things get out of control before they come to accept the facts, assuming they ever do.

They have been treating this like any other outbreak scenario and it is killing everyone. Some nations might arrive at the right solutions faster than others, but the damage will still be severe, especially considering that those in charge in the faraway places like that are usually the first to receive new vaccinations.

"It will be a miracle if border conflicts or even outright war isn't on the horizon," Miles mutters, mostly to himself. Hewitt shakes his head as the same line of reasoning is triggered by Miles' comment.

"We're fucked if we can't get ahead of this thing and get a vaccine developed, a real vaccine," Mariah says. "That is the only way we can hope to stop the spread of this madness."

Hewitt replies from the backseat, "Gale couldn't work out a vaccine, and he was the genius who created this monster in the first place."

"Was Gale ever really trying to develop a cure, though?" Mariah asks, voicing the question they all carried in the back of their minds ever since Gale's startling revelations.

'Honestly, I don't know if I believe he was," Hewitt acknowledges, after a short pause to consider his most sincere thoughts on the matter.

"I spent a great deal of time poring through his research these last few days," he continues, "and I couldn't find any recent work on a vaccine, and nothing at all that would lead me to believe he was actively trying to counteract the illness or mitigate the effects. This was his fucking baby, and he was so proud of it that I don't think he could bear to kill it."

No one has a response. There is nothing else to say. Miles silently resumes driving and they continue down the road, somber, staring out the windows at the peaceful and beautiful landscape that belies the horrible realities they will be confronting soon enough.

Another five minutes pass before Hewitt speaks again, "Miles, I need you to stop the car."

"Are you feeling alright?" Mariah asks, concern in her voice.

"What the fuck are you talking about?" Miles replies, seeing the expression on his friend's face in the rearview mirror and knowing it has nothing to do with feeling ill.

"I need to go back," he says in response.

"What do you mean, you need to go back?"

Hewitt takes a deep breath. "I need to get back into Gale's research and get back to work where he left off when he was working on the vaccine."

Mariah speaks up from the passenger seat, "You're no virologist and you certainly aren't a world-class molecular biologist like Gale was."

"No, I'm not. But I do have enough education to know what Gale was working on and he fastidiously documented everything."

"Do you honestly believe you can figure something out?" Miles finally asks, his tone not mocking or derisive but hopeful.

"I do."

"We are not letting you go back there, Hewitt," Mariah insists, tears welling up in her eyes as she stares at him from the passenger seat, her neck craned awkwardly to look at him. "This conversation is over."

"I need to go back," he says.

"Well," Mariah replies, "I need you with me."

He doesn't have a response to that, so Hewitt closes his mouth.

52

CHAPTER FIFTY-TWO

THEY CONTINUE DRIVING IN silence for another couple of minutes.

"I can't go with you," Hewitt speaks up loudly from the back seat, surprising everyone with the certainty of his tone. His eyes never waver from Mariah's.

"What in the fuck are you talking about?" Miles asks, his tone exasperated and unbelieving. "Where the hell else are you planning on going, because you are not going back that way? That place is dead, brother, it's a graveyard."

Hewitt thinks for a moment, trying to put his thoughts into a coherent enough state to express them before answering, "I think that I should go back to Gale's lab. There's something there, something in his notes or research, something that can be used to stop what he started."

"You pored over all of it, you said so yourself," Mariah pleads, tears running down her cheeks. "There was nothing there."

"We have to stick together, asshole. You know that," Miles replies.

Catching a glimpse of Hewitt's expression in the rearview mirror, Miles slows the car to a stop, shaking his head the whole time. Miles offers to turn around and get Hewitt back to the lab, but Hewitt insists he can walk from where they are. He argues that they'd already lost too much time. He doesn't want to delay them any further than he already has.

Mariah, finally stopping the flow of tears from her eyes and embraces him, wondering if she will ever see Hewitt again after this. He is plagued by similar thoughts but refuses to give voice to them, thinking that doing so will only make that outcome more likely than it surely is. She takes his cheeks in the palms of her hands, locking eyes with him for a few seconds, silently imploring him to change his mind. Something she sees there tells her there's no point in arguing, and she kisses him. The kiss is desperate, passionate, imbued with all the things neither of them can bring themselves to say out loud.

When Mariah finally pulls away and lets her hands slide from his face, Hewitt is almost convinced to change his mind—almost. He smiles at her, nods his head, and hopes that she can read his mind, because he'll break down if he tries to put anything he's thinking into words.

"You should probably keep the kid here with you," Miles suggests as Hewitt shakes his hand. "It's going to be safer here with you, plus Mariah and I will make better time if we just have to watch each other's backs."

Hewitt turns to look at Ben, and the boy silently nods his head.

"That works for me," he says. "I might need some assistance anyhow and we have plenty of supplies left in town to hold out for a long goddamn time, just the two of us."

"If we come across any clean survivors on the road, we'll send them back your way with any additional things they can haul with them," Mariah suggests.

"That's an excellent plan," Hewitt responds, his eyes lighting up as he considers the possibilities. "There are plenty of smaller communities where they wouldn't have been getting the vaccines Gale had tampered with."

He pauses for a moment, his eyes glazed as he loses himself in thought.

"They more than likely would have been listening to the same kind of broadcasts we've heard, though," he continues. "Maybe convincing them that holing up somewhere more defensible wouldn't be a bad idea."

Ben and Hewitt remain standing in the middle of the road watching the SUV with its trailer until it passes out of sight around the bend. Just like that, the two of them are the only living people left in the region, and Hewitt's last two surviving friends have just disappeared from sight. Hopeful as he tries to be, he can't contain the shiver that runs from head to toes.

Hewitt pats the boy on the back and says, "Well, young man, we've got a bit of a hike ahead of us. Let's get going."

Together, they walk back down the road toward the town they'd only just escaped. Neither of them knows whether they will ever see another living human being again after this, but they both understand that they need to have faith in Miles and Mariah to successfully make it out there with the information they have.

Maybe they can get some experts, perhaps even some former colleagues of Gale's, who could make use of the plethora of research data in the lab. Hewitt knows that he will welcome any extra sets of eyes because he is going to be out of his depth; as smart as he might be, he only has so much education that will benefit him in this. He still intends to dig through the records and files as if it all depends on him to find a solution because it could very well still come down to that.

"Before we go back to the lab, what do you think of heading to Gale's house for some lunch that isn't canned or dehydrated?" Hewitt asks.

"That sounds great to me," Ben replies without hesitation, smiling.

Gale's kitchen is fully stocked and the important things, refrigeration, and electronics, never lost power thanks to what must have been an enormous back-up generator. Over the last few days, the four survivors had been altogether too busy to spend any time digging through Gale's kitchen, which works out well for Hewitt and Ben.

The two of them will be able to enjoy at least one good meal every day for the next week or two until expiration dates start to tick past. Under the current circumstances, it's the little things that can make the unbearable almost tolerable, and the two of them have a lot of little things to be thankful for.

53

CHAPTER FIFTY-THREE

MILES AND MARIAH BOTH keep an eye on Hewitt and Ben in the rearview mirror until they finally pass the curve that takes them out of sight. They each exhale a sigh, almost as if it's been choreographed.

The road stretches out ahead of them, a path leading directly into an unfolding apocalypse that there was never any chance of avoiding. They drive with the radio on, panic in the voices of reporters as they document the decline of civilization, the virus spreading like a conflagration through cities and suburbs and spilling out into more rural locations.

The sun is high, almost directly above the car as Miles speeds them along Southwest, desperately hoping to reach Ben's mother before she too is consumed by this new pandemic. They had made a promise to the boy and his late father, and both Miles and Mariah intended to keep that promise no matter how much of a risk there might be in doing so. The bright, warm spring day does nothing to ease the sensation that they are driving into a darkness that might consume them, along with the rest of the world.

In the passenger seat, Mariah field strips a 9mm and continues from there to loading extra magazines for the three handguns they are carrying with them. The shotgun and rifle are loaded and sitting on the back seat. Wrapped in a blanket in the trunk is the MP5 that Miles carries with him at all times, along with numerous other supplies, including a great deal of the surplus ammunition they collected from the town. They both know that they aren't adequately equipped for what they are rushing towards at close to 90MPH, but neither of them cares to consider their odds consciously.

With Hewitt and Ben remaining behind in a town devoid of life, sealed in the same laboratory where the virus was developed, there was at least some small chance of a cure being discovered. Mariah knows that she has something to return to, even if they fail in the mission that they are on. Whether Hewitt fails or succeeds in finding a cure, she wants to be there with him, especially if this is the end of the world.

It's a matter of faith at this point, nothing more concrete than that, faith that they will see those two again and that they won't all just end up dead very soon. Miles, always the soldier, can focus on an objective and narrow that focus until nothing will distract him from that one thing. Mariah, on the other hand, having spent her adult life fixated on various concepts of the end times, has already been battling a nihilistic voice in the back of her mind, a voice that tells her to go back to Hewitt and live out the rest of whatever life they might have in the relative safety of the now-empty town.

It is difficult not to interpret the empty roads as a bad sign, but these same mountain roads had been virtually empty on the way there as well. There are signs of activity, finally, as they begin crossing through high elevation valleys and meadows that have been converted into farms and ranches.

As they pass a field with workers laboring under the late morning sun, they decide they will stop and check things out. Neither the laborers nor the family who owns the plot appear to be suffering any ill effects and they've been remaining isolated here while they wait for the news from the rest of the country to change perspective to something more positive. They recommend establishing contact with Hewitt and keeping their eyes open for either more survivors or people displaying symptoms of infection.

They determine they will stop at any of these homes that appear to be safe and occupied since these nearby locations could be the surest option for resources needed by survivors as they gather in the town. Many of the ranchers had heard the same radio broadcasts and already knew that the world outside of their isolated little pocket had gone to shit. Some of them met Miles and Mariah with skepticism, having not heard the news for themselves, but they are convinced once they tune into those stations.

Leaving out the fact that they'd been friends with the mad genius behind this whole catastrophe, the condensed version of their story they told leads locals to believe that they had been here on some official, government-sanctioned investigation. Miles reinforces this by introducing himself with his former rank and Mariah as a doctor, never mind that her Ph.D. was a liberal arts degree.

The locals all agree to be alert, all of them owning firearms of their own and comfortable using them as necessary. More importantly, they agree to reach out to other neighbors further off the beaten path and to remain vigilant for survivors being sent their way. Arguably, as far as Mariah is concerned, the most important part is that they will establish contact with Hewitt and Ben at the lab and offer any assistance they can provide for those two.

Distracted, Hewitt certainly still manages to sound relieved to hear the good news when Mariah radios back to him to let him know that there are healthy survivors outside in the rest of the world, even if they're likely to be found only in isolated agrarian communities. This will be the final radio broadcast she's able to share with Hewitt, as they are quickly pushing against the range limit of the late deputy's equipment.

Miles reassures everyone they encounter that there are bound to be plenty of uninfected survivors in the cities and small towns all over the country as well as in these outlying communities. Not everyone received their shots and certainly, there would be a good many folks who had the skills or blind luck required to make it unscathed through paranoid mobs and apparent zombies.

What Miles neglects to mention is his concern that military personnel, government employees, first responders, and hospital staff were traditionally the first to receive new vaccinations when there was some new illness on the rise. His worry, exacerbated by things he was listening for and wasn't hearing in the radio broadcasts, is that there could be no organized or well-equipped relief effort underway anywhere.

This unspoken fear dovetails with his other major concern, that those most well trained and armed will have been the first to turn against others. He tries to push these thoughts aside because the prospect makes the whole situation more horrifying than it already was.

A little bit of hope and positivity here, in the beginning, might count for something and it does seem to help a bit for the people they speak with.

WITH ALL THE STOPS along the way, it takes them until the following morning before they can see signs that they are approaching Spokane in the distance. They'd taken turns sleeping for a couple of hours each, Miles finally waking Mariah just before dawn so that they could begin their journey again.

They choose not to stop at any further homes since they started back on the road at sunrise. The seeds had been sewn with the neighboring farmers and they would do their part in building lines of communication and establishing contact with others who are safe.

It's time to see how badly more urban population centers had fared. They finally join up with Interstate 90 between Coeur d'Alene and Spokane, just past the Washington side of the border. Things already look ugly.

Wrecks line patches of the roadway and there is a smoke haze in the air from fires either still burning or only recently extinguished and left to shoulder. There is occasional furtive movement in the peripheral of what they can see, but no aggression right away.

Mariah may have never so much as entertained the thought of enlisting with the military, but she and Miles are in sync. Both of them have firearms locked and loaded and their heads on a swivel. Things are going to get worse before they get better. Both of them are well aware of this; neither of them even attempts to speculate just how much worse things will be getting and they choose not to breathe life into the suspicion that things might never get back to being better.

"If you've got a third eye, open that motherfucker," Miles mutters. "If you have eyes in the back of your head, keep 'em wide."

"What's that you're saying?" Mariah asks.

"Just some bullshit one of my superiors used to say when we were heading into the shit back in Afghanistan, something to do with calling on any resources in preparation for the difficulty of keeping yourself alive," Miles replies, chuckling a little. "If ever anyone has dived right into the shit, it's us, right fucking now. It just seemed appropriate."

"Definitely."

Miles nods solemnly. "Let's get into that shit, then."

Author's Notes & Acknowledgments

When I self-published Innocence Ends in August of 2020, it was a story two decades in the making. It seems only appropriate that it ultimately founds its way into the world during a real-life pandemic. And now, another few years have passed.

Nothing about the creation of this novel was linear. Sporadically, I would find myself fixating on a scene, and I'd do my best to flesh it out and get it written, only for the manuscript to go back on hiatus—sometimes for months, sometimes for years—until another scene began playing out behind my eyes. Rinse and repeat. For more than half of the twenty years I worked on this book, this was the process.

It all began with a conversation between my old friend James and I, back in 1998 or 1999. We were talking about some tropes we loved in B-horror flicks; mad scientists, vacations gone wrong, small towns with dark secrets, zombies, battling against the environment, and so on. We wanted to see these elements thrown together, but not as a gag or some low-budget romp. It was about telling a story that handled these individual aspects with the love and appreciation he and I both felt for them. I like to think I've managed to do that here.

Along the way, certain elements were changed or discarded, and the story that started germinating during that conversation has evolved into the version you have in your hands. There's a lot of truth in these pages, hidden amid the fiction—potentially more than you might think. Many of the activities the characters participated in during their youth are the same things my friends and I enjoyed during our teen years.

Of course, we dedicated countless hours to watching horror movies, playing horror-themed video games, and fantasizing about the impending zombie apocalypse—and how it might come to pass in real life. It was a regular thing for us; finding our way into abandoned buildings, construction sites, onto downtown rooftops, and other places we didn't belong.

We explored. We trespassed. We split into smaller groups and spent our nights hunting each other through alleys and virtually empty commercial neighborhoods.

These were some of the best nights of my life, and it felt like we would always be friends at the time. While that wasn't how it played out in real life, I made sure it worked out that way for the fictional assortment of friends populating the story you've presumably just finished reading. Aspects of some of my old friends (only a couple of whom are still part of my life) may have found their way into the characters you've followed through their own apocalyptic experiences. Elements of myself are in there too.

The "End of the World" soundtrack Hewitt listens to throughout the book consists of some songs I have on a themed playlist of my own. The playlist in question was often what I was listening to while working on the manuscript back in late 2019 and early 2020, when I was finally completing the decades-long labor of love.

In many ways, this book is a tribute to the years my group of friends spent together. This book would not exist if not for Joel, James, Nick, Carl, Michael, Heather, and all the people who came and went during our nocturnal adventures. No matter how we've changed or grown apart, my memories of those years are still some of my favorites.

The odds are good that this book also wouldn't exist if it weren't for the numerous people who let me bounce ideas off of them as I discussed the story I wanted to tell. I owe all of them a great deal of gratitude. I owe you as well, for taking the time to read what I've written.

I'd wanted to include an Author's Note in the original publication of this novel, but it felt self-indulgent, and I was certain no one would care about anything I had to say about the personal history behind the scenes. This new release allows me to correct that error, since it seems the notes I've incorporated along with many of my stories are welcome additions, according to multiple readers.

I'm grateful for Candace Nola taking such an active interest in this book, and asking me if I would be willing to work with her on a new, improved edition. Her faith in me and her enthusiastic belief in the story I'd crafted gave me an opportunity to repair a couple of minor issues—hopefully making it a slightly better story than the earlier release. It also gave me a chance to share these thoughts with you.

I'm also grateful to Carver Pike, who helped motivate me to release Innocence Ends back in 2020. I met him during the KillerCon virtual event in August of that year. Talking with him about his experiences with self-publishing—and hearing his encouragement—was the impetus that pushed me to take the leap and put this story out into the world.

And I would be remiss if I didn't express gratitude to Lisa Lee Tone, the first person to review the original edition of this novel. I also had the pleasure of meeting her thanks to that same KillerCon event, and it was because of her that I found a home for another couple titles with Madness Heart Press, and the uniquely bizarre family John Baltisberger has assembled under that publishing house.

—Nikolas P. Robinson

June 2024

— · —

ALSO BY NIKOLAS P. ROBISON

UNSPOKEN
   Errata: Collected Short Fiction & Poetry
   You Will Be Consumed
   May Cause Unexplained Ocular Bleeding
   Beneath the Unspoiled Wilderness
   Dog Days: The Complete Lee Melvin Collection

Short Fiction on Godless
Horseplay
Daemonica
Where Dreams Come True
Have You Seen Me?
When You're Here, You're Fatalities
Dog Days
Dog Days: The Hunt
The Cold-Blooded Hills
Hounds of War
Dog Days: The Bridge

With Elizabeth J. McKee
Nativity

With Candace Nola, Eric Butler, & M. Ennenbach
The Generator

9 798893 990072